WHISPER

WHISPER

Fran Dobbie

Hodder Headline Australia

This is a work of fiction. Any resemblance of the characters to people alive or dead is entirely coincidental.

This project has been assisted by the Commonwealth Government through the Australia Council, its arts funding and advisory body.

A Mark Macleod Book

Published in Australia and New Zealand in 2000
by Hodder Headline Australia Pty Limited
(A member of the Hodder Headline Group)
Level 22, 201 Kent Street, Sydney NSW 2000
Website: www.hha.com.au

**National Library of Australia
Cataloguing-in-Publication data**

Dobbie, Fran.
  Whisper.

  ISBN 0 7336 1207 5.

  1. Aborigines, Australian - Families - Fiction.
  2. Friendship - Fiction. 3. Aborigines, Australian - Fiction. 4. Short stories, Australian. I. Title.

A823.4

Text design by Danielle Cairis
Typesetting by Bookhouse, Sydney
Printed in Australia by Griffin Press, Adelaide

For those who allow me to fly:
Troy
Joel
Peter
Mum
Dad
X

Contents

Acknowledgments

Within the pages of these stories are many memories and shared experiences. I would like to thank all those special people who have encouraged and influenced me while writing this, my first book. Love to Melanie and Lisa (without you both Maggie would not be); my inspiring and insightful agent, Selwa; Peta (thanks for the window to my stories); Mark and everyone at Hodder; Leanne, David and Andrew; and all my blessed nieces and nephews. John and Clare and family, Clarkie (what talent), Elena , Ross, Glenis, Liz, Lynece, Geoff, Peter, Mumoross, Uncle Lloyd and Daisy, Aunty Dawn and family, Uncle Tom, Aunty Diane and family, Brian, Leanne, Justine, Father Mac, Matthew, Belinda, Lisa, Patrick, Jean, Linda, Mal and Maryann.

To all the children I have taught, your spirit and sense of fun put vitality into the stories.

Lauren, Luke, Emma, Hayley, Laura, Emma, Blake, Cameron, Jessie, Jo-Anne, Lizzy, Brenda, Margaret and Penny. Aunty Marg and family, Angie, Aunty Sylvia and family, Rita, Sisters Ann and Veronica.

To all my friends I didn't mention: you know who you are. Your friendship has inspired my path to writing.

And lastly, to those who have journeyed home: Melissa, Uncle Billy, Chris, Terry, Uncle Cyril, Wendy, George and Jordan.

Thank you.

EDIE'S DREAM

I had this dream...

'Hey, Aunty, is there any biscuits cookin'?' I said. I'm Edith Ann. How proper! Most folks call me Edie, and that's my Aunty Gwen. She's raising me. You know, she's really my nanna but I call her Aunty. I've got a special friend, Maggie. Maggie and I, we're such good friends. She comes from the other side of the river and we meet every day down by the creek. Maggie's much taller than I am and we laugh and we yarn: story after story. She's good value.

'Hey, you girls! Out you go, outside and play. Those biscuits will be coming soon,' says

Aunty Gwen. Let me tell you about her. Have you ever met a person who, even when you sit in the silence and speak no words, can say so much and make you feel safe and sort of loved and "at home"? You know that feeling?

Aunty's married to Uncle Tom (Pop). You see, my mum didn't want me. She left, and only the boys went with her. I think she had it tough so it was easier to leave. I'm glad in a way.

I've got a great life. I'm free, we live on a farm and I've got a heap of room to run and get lost in. I'm always thinking and dreaming, I suppose. Sometimes I go on the most excellent trips.

'Edie, are you coming? Let's go and get some slime to throw at Old Sam's cows. See if we can scare them away from the waterhole so we can catch some yabbies,' says Maggie. 'Hurry up, girl!' And she shoves me to wake up.

Running through the air and just missing Old Sam's wooden barriers, sliding through the lush green grass and rolling down the embankment to our camp. No one can find us here. Our hideout's got homemade weapons and traps to protect us from those people, those people in the shiny black cars.

'Over here,' Maggie says. Our slime is thick, juicy green oozy stuff.

'Get that stick over there,' I say. 'It's chunky; it'll do the trick!' There's a special way to make our slimeys. You twirl three times to the right and then two times back and the same again. This makes it tight and strong and just what you need to scare those overfed black and white cows.

'Are you ready, Maggs?' I say.

'Yes, let's get 'em!' she says, flying through the air, slimeys everywhere. 'Great shot!' Maggie shouts as she runs towards the hole.

'Watch out, they're moving!' BANG! 'Oh no! Old Sam's heard us!' I yell, and Maggs and I run back to our hideout. Puffed out, we've got to have a rest.

Even though Old Sam's a cranky old man I just know he would not hurt us. You know, I saw him one day rocking Toby, his grandson, on his front porch after he'd had an awful fall and cut his leg. He was singing to him and I couldn't believe it.

Suddenly we hear *that* bell ringing: it's Pop's way to alert us to trouble, and you can hear it clear across the river. We know what we have to do.

'Quick! To the dead people's home!' I yell. That's the cemetery where all my kin are resting.

Like frisbees flying through the air, we're there, safe. I can hardly get my breath but I know I can't make any noise.

'Edie, are you right?' Maggie whispers.

'Yes. Can you see them?' I say.

'They're talking to Uncle, so don't move,' she says quietly. Another long, quiet wait. Those trees become our friends, they protect us from something we don't quite understand.

The old folks won't let us hear the talk. They go for walks and come back sad, just like a raindrop falling from a cloud, lost until it touches the ground, its home. We sit and sit and sit. Darkness—I don't like the cold!

'Listen, Maggs. It's the bird,' I say. We always know it's safe once we hear that bird.

'Aunty's calling us, Edie. Ssmmeeeeeellll that stew!' says Maggie. Aunty's stews are famous for bringing folks home, so we climb down, knowing that everything is fine now.

What a sight: Pop sitting on the porch playing his harmonica and Aunty stirring and stirring.

'Go in and wash those hands because it's time to eat,' says Aunty Gwen. She stands there smiling, a sad kind of smile. 'Hurry up now, you two!' What a special lady my aunty is. Maggie always stays over at my home when the bell rings. It always seems to be a long wait when the black car comes calling, so her folks and mine agree it's best for her to stay and they'll get her in the morning.

Another day, another adventure. We always have lots of them.

When I grow up, you know, my adventures will be safe and free and take me to places where I am the same as everyone and I don't have to be scared no more!

I've got this dream...

EDIE'S
FORGET-ME-NOT

There's a place that's secret where no one goes, but there are three words there. It's beside the creek: there are two big rocks standing separate, just like kings or something. They have this awesome power.

I always wondered what was behind those kings, so I told Aunty and she said that I mustn't go lookin' because I might find trouble. I didn't know what she meant by that. How could rocks cause you trouble? Anyway, this particular day I called by to see my friend Maggs and told her about this place.

'Let's go and see what's behind them rocks,' she said. Maggie was always a bit more game than me at exploring.

'Okay, let's go and see the kings, but we'll have to wear our boots because there might be a lot of mountain climbing,' I said.

Off we went running free, the air blowing knots into my hair. I hate it, but Aunty always says that folks would love to have my hair. I reckon if they want mine they can have it; I'd rather have long, flowing hair like Maggs because she hardly ever gets tangles.

Anyway it was spring here and there were new flowers everywhere and heaps of butter-flies. I wished I was a butterfly just doin' whatever I wanted...

'Come on, Edie. Stop dreaming, girl! Keep up: you're too slow!' Maggie yelled way in front of me.

Finally we saw the kings. 'Wow, Edie! They're real big. How come we never found them before?' she said.

''Cause we spend too much time up Tommo's side of the creek,' I said. Maggie stood there staring, frozen in her boots and as white as the moon on a hot summer's night.

'Move it, you chicken! Nothin' can harm us! This is our land and remember what Aunty and Pop always say: our kin's spirits will protect us,' I reminded her. I must admit I'd never seen Maggs spooked before except when those people came askin' for me, and that was sort of a game. You were scared but it didn't seem real. It just happened.

'Let's have a smokin',' I said. Maggs moved slowly as we picked up sticks and leaves and rocks. You see, when you sit within the smoke it covers you like a blanket and takes care of your spirit. I have lots of them.

We crept through the kings like a snake slithering slowly. 'Oooh!' we gasped.

'It's like Adam and Eve's garden that Aunty read to me about,' I said.

'It's beautiful, Edie. There's a fern bed and all,' Maggie exclaimed.

'See, girl, this is a kind place. Listen to the wind whispering,' I whispered.

We sat a long while.

'You know, this place reminds me of my

mum: warm and safe and so, so beautiful,' sighed Maggie. I started to cry. 'What's wrong, Edie? I didn't mean for you to cry,' she said.

You see, my mum died and we only got the word and I didn't tell Maggie. I thought she'd think I was stupid. I was thirteen years old and I didn't even know my mum. She left me when I was young, for good reasons I'm sure.

'Edie, let's never come here again. Just leave it the way it is, untouched,' Maggs said, with her hand touching me lightly.

We walked the earth silently, silently back home.

I learnt something that special day: that the love of a mother is a gift from God whether you know her or you don't. She was given to me to learn from and to start me on my journey in life and to make my journey better than hers.

Forget-me-not.

I go on many adventures but none can mean more than carving those three special words.

BACKYARD
MEMORIES

It was that time of year again. Christmas holidays were here and everybody was in high spirits. Downtown everything was on the move, with people buying last-minute goodies. I loved it, it smelt just delicious. Now this time of year brought many families home, and ours was no exception. Cousins, friends and family came from all over. They just turned up. I don't know how Aunty fed them all, but she always managed. The hamper arrived from Mr Parsons' shop as usual the day before, because Aunty said that it always pays to be prepared! Everyone was happy, but getting together specially brought a shine to my heart.

Parcels were given to Pop and they were filled with love, Aunty would often say: 'Bits and pieces of love given from the heart.' I didn't realise what she was saying until later. I like to draw, so with Pop's help I made frames and glued my drawings to them. I really enjoyed making each one of my parcels of love, and I understood what she meant.

Outside the front door were placed two potted pine trees, and all year they were pruned and lovingly cared for by Pop. This was one of our special traditions. Each year would bring a new baby into our big family, and a handmade decoration was made by the baby's mother and hung on one of the trees. Both trees were full. And as you walked into our home everything was sweet and pretty. Oh, how I loved Christmas!

'Edie, go and fetch some pine cones and take the girls with you,' yelled Pop.

'Okay, Missy, Jo: let's go.' I grabbed their collars, we jumped the back fence and, before you could wink, we were down along the creek picking up cones.

'I can outrun you, Edie. Catch me if you can,' Missy said, whipping past me with her long, wavy locks.

Before we knew it our shirts were full. We decided to rest our hands and sit beneath the old shady pine. Yarning deeply, we hadn't noticed the rain gently misting our hair.

'Look, girls,' Jo said, 'a jimmy's coming.' A jimmy was the name we gave to a storm cloud. We made up lots of different names and the old folks didn't know what we were saying because it was our code. Well, the jimmy appeared from nowhere and before we stood up, it was rattling its stuff.

'Get out from under the tree!' I yelled. 'Down here!' I pointed to a hole in the side of the creek bed. 'We can hide here until it passes.' The hole was just big enough and we sat, it seemed like forever, but it wasn't easing. The creek water started to move quickly and our toes got wet. Now I was frightened, and I could feel Missy's heart pumping at my elbow. She was only nine and she was starting to cry.

'We're going to drown and I want to go home,' she sobbed into my shoulder.

'Don't be silly,' Jo said. 'They'll come.'

And as the words left her mouth we heard Pop calling out, 'Edie, Missy, Jo!' He must have heard Missy's sobs and with the help of some of the others, reached over the bank and pulled us out. They wrapped blankets around us and took us home. By the time we arrived the rain had stopped.

'You girls dry off and change,' Aunty Lizzy said, as she hustled the three of us through the door.

'Funny weather of late,' Pop said. He looked up and scratched his head. But with the excitement over, the afternoon continued, with the trestle tables laid out and all the smells of the season tantalising everyone.

Folks came days before Christmas and seemed to stay long after, and they all brought something to share. We went exploring. Some of my aunties and uncles took us to collect bush berries and dig for yams. You could see my cousins in those wattle trees peeling the bark away from the sap—its sweet, yummy gum. Pop's friends had already gathered, skinned, prepared and stored the meat in the cooler. Laughter was shared, and a smile just seemed to cross the earth. Evening was filled with song and dance and as the stars scattered the darkness, sleeping bodies lay warmly enjoying the vastness of the night sky.

On Christmas Eve, we went to church, the whole lot of us and it was something! Sleep was easy that night. If I didn't go to sleep, Santa wouldn't bring that special present. Staring out my window, I wondered what it would be.

'Please make it big,' I whispered into the night. I rolled over, happy for the knee in my back and the foot up my nose because it was Christmas and we were all together!

After our sharing, the women prepared lunch. 'Edie, take a seat here!' I looked up and there was Aunty Kat, those dark beady eyes and round rimmed glasses summoning me to sit beside her. *Oh no*, I thought, *not this year*. Every year she sat beside me and watched my manners, tapping me over the head or the hands with her silver spoon.

'I'm fine, Aunty. I'll sit next to Jo,' I said

politely, making a quick dive for the opposite side of the table.

'Come on, love, over here,' she said very loudly. 'You're my favourite,' she persisted. I pretended I didn't hear her and went to sit down beside Jo.

'Move over, quick!' I whispered in her ear.

'Here she comes, Edie. Sit on the edge,' Jo said, gently pushing me. 'She's too big. Don't worry. The old cow...moooo!' Jo said, giggling. We were a pair, us two. We didn't see each other often, but when we did, trouble had a double "b" in it.

'Now, now, now.' Aunty Kat just grabbed a chair and sat at the head of the table. I rolled my eyes, tutted and she heard me, and within a moment, I got a tap on the head. Jo reckoned if we could get her glasses we could roll them in the dirt, scratch them and then partly cut through the wire leading to her hearing box and she'd never find us! So on it went every Christmas: Aunty Kat told us the same old stories every, every year, and we just had to listen.

'Backyard memories,' Aunty said. 'They

belong to you. They make you. YOU!' And she poked a finger softly into my chest.

But one Christmas she didn't come. Aunty Gwen said that Aunty Kat had finally packed her bag for the last time and that her beautiful long eyelashes were now gently brushing the dust fairies away. A smile touched her lips. Aunty Kat was happily going home.

I didn't realise it then, but her stories were to become my backyard memories too.

SOUL FOOD

Have you ever owned something so important to you that it is etched into your heart? Something that becomes a part of who you are and that you take through your life to share with others? Sometimes it even hurts!

'Hear the wind? It's gathering up the earth, and breathing its very soul into you, girl. Can you feel its message?' These words echo through my mind. Aunty Gwen said it was the Great Creator's gift to us, just like blood flowing through our veins. I did not always understand her yarns, but I listened. Aunty was a wise old woman.

Long white rays of light peeped through folds of material above my head and I kept staring at them to see the dust fairies dance across my room, as I lay listening to my bird friend Willywagtail summoning me to come and sing with him. They're sacred, Pop always said. I lay there for as long as I could, hoping Aunty would forget to wake me for school! But she never forgot. I had chores to do, the hens needed feeding. I had to gather their eggs from the night before and pump the water needed for boiling, every single morning. I thought I had a hard life.

Across the field I could see Pop looking after his vegies, digging and whistling. 'Morning, Edie!' he'd say, as the breeze brought his words to my ears.

When I'd finished my chores, Aunty would tell me to come and sit down. I always had a big feed every morning.

'Now, Edie, I want you to go to Maggs's place today after school and stay there until I come for you,' she said one day.

'Why?' I asked.

'Because your pop and I have some matters

to attend to.' Some matters! I decided I didn't want to know, as her words had a sort of strange feel to them.

'Okay, but can I take my boots, so Maggs and I can go exploring?' I begged.

'Yes, but don't go near the back paddocks,' she said firmly.

'Why not, Aunty? That's where the best spots are for tadpoling and—'

'Not today!' she said.

'Okay, maybe tomorrow,' I said under my breath.

School was boring. Miss Pit never smiled and there were always her little beady eyes behind those glasses and her long wooden pointer, tap, tap, tapping on the board. 'Now, class! Today...'

And that's where I left her: I was off on another journey. I wondered what Maggie's mum was cooking for dinner. And before I knew it, the bell was calling us home.

'Let's go to Old Sam's place!' Maggs shouted, running just two fence palings ahead of me. You see, Old Sam, he was getting soft. We visited him every couple of days, and there he was, waiting with hot scones and butter, just like he knew we would be there, almost as if he wanted us to come. We'd sit, we'd yarn, he'd curse someone, and we'd go. But this day he left a sour feeling in our minds.

'There's trouble in town. So stay away, you girls, and don't ask. Just stay away!' he said angrily.

Maggs raced past me to get the lead. 'See ya, Old Sam!' we yelled. We didn't have to say much to each other. Friends just know. We were off to catch some taddies.

The smell of the creek would draw you to her. You could feel her coolness on your skin. There was life in her flowing movement, and peace was what she gave us.

'Watch out, Edie!' Maggs screamed. And before I knew it, I was down. 'It's those skinny ankles you've got,' she said. I hadn't seen the log and now my ankle was the size of a potato.

'I'm going to die,' I moaned.

'I'll get those leaves that Aunty said will take the swelling out,' Maggs said, and I started to cry. Within minutes she was back. 'Here, I've found some.' She wrapped the wet leaves on my fat potato. 'You'll be right. I'll take you home, but don't tell Mum where we were. Okay?'

'Why?' I asked.

'Because of the land, your land. It's not our business, she said to Dad.'

'What land?' I asked.

'All she said was that it was so sad,' Maggs said quietly. We could hear a howling noise crossing the creek, and on the rise we saw some people with papers, cursing each other.

'Edie, it's Pop and Aunty,' Maggie whispered. Something was wrong and I could feel it. *Matters to attend to*, I thought. And Maggie found me a fork stick. The wind carried the howling noise and it followed us home.

They came and took some of our land and I knew then that my grandmother would never be the same.

Aunty came for me that night. Maggie's mum and dad spoke to her for a long time, then they drove us home in silence. My ankle didn't take long to mend and I was back running the earth as if it had never happened. All Pop said to me was, 'A part of what feeds our souls has been taken, but our spirit will never leave, as our essence lives within it and it belongs to us.'

Other folks didn't keep up with their bills, but they were given a chance to save what was theirs. The people said the land was needed for future development, and why did two old people need so much anyway? *But what about me?* I thought. *That land was mine too!*

It was rooted deep in our hearts, to be shared and nurtured and for all to grow from. Can you feel it and hear it? It's breathing its very soul into you. How do you take something that is already owned? It doesn't belong; it just is!

THE SHELL

They came into town, in a vehicle loaded for adventure. Were they staying? Who could say! Their energy and laughter still live among the waves, and every shell Maggs and I collected speaks their names.

The water crashed against the rocks and left traces of sparkling gold, the magic wonder of the sea. She drew many to her, each with their own reason for being a part of her strength. *Did she give it to them?* I wondered. This was my place to just be. You could look far into the distance and see her smile reflect the sky above. All summer long, we ventured on down to her shores. Maggie and I would make enormous sandcastles, usually away from the crowd of people flocking to swim there.

'We're getting too old to build these,' Maggie said.

'I know, but don't you think we're being creative? Like Miss Pit said at school, it's the "ESSENCE OF OUR SOUL".' I said it in a loud, dramatic voice.

'Suppose so...' she said, as she rolled her laughing eyes at me. Aunty said more folks needed to find this essence, after I told her what Miss Pit had said. 'It warms the soul,' she said.

'What are you kids making?' A strong male voice came from behind us, and surprised us as we flicked back our stringy wet hair.

'You scared us!' Maggie said. I just sat there staring. Where had he come from?

'Sorry,' he said. 'Looks good. Can I join you?' Shrugging, we indicated he could help, but no one spoke for a while as an uneasy feeling came between Maggs and me. We never spoke to strangers, but he seemed to have a friendly air about him.

The castle now seemed so silly. 'What are

your names?' he asked, patting away at the
sand wall.

'I'm Maggie and this is Edie,' Maggs said
rudely. I didn't know why she was so angry.

'Hi, I'm Chris. My friends and I are just
passing through, on a surfing mission,' he said.

'What's a surfing mission?' I asked.

'We try and find our soul and...'

'Well, shouldn't you look for it somewhere
else?' Maggie said sarcastically, shaking her
hair from side to side. I didn't know what had
got into her. I'd never seen this side of Maggie
before!

'We're just surfing and having fun!' he said,
smiling as a breeze caught and swept his
golden curls lightly across his face.

'Where do you live?' I asked.

'Under the stars and in our cars,' he whispered. He didn't seem to mind that Maggs was
annoyed by his just being there. He was enjoying the moment. In no time at all the wet sand
was transformed into a lost city with channels
and caves and shells for windows. Pretty good
for beginners, really. But without any warning,
suddenly he was gone.

'What's got into you? You were so rude to that guy. He was only trying to help and be friendly,' I said angrily.

'I don't know. For starters he scared me, and I don't like talking to strange people, especially surfers,' Maggs said.

'Why? They're like anyone else, just enjoying for a short time what we have always,' I said more calmly.

We walked home along the rocks in silence. Maggie was really angry at me; you could have cut the air with a knife. I just started talking to myself and pretending that she would answer and maybe come around.

I was having an interesting conversation when suddenly I realised that she had stopped three rocks back, and was sitting there, staring out to sea. Time passed as I left her in her space on the rocks.

'You know, Edie, Rod never came home,' she said quietly. I knew her brother's name was Rodney and that he had left. Aunty said so. I came closer and just listened.

Rod was years older than Maggie. He loved the water and would surf from early morning

29

on and you could see his silhouette gliding across the moon as it surfaced above the water. He was wild and yet peaceful, something his parents couldn't understand. He was always alone, yet he was never lonely.

One day he met some boys from out of town, and got into some kind of trouble. The twinkle was gone from his eyes and the life drained from his face. What went wrong? No one knew. He just disappeared as if sliding over the moon to the other side. That was his parents' pain, and the heartache was shared by a little girl in nappies.

We sat in silence, watching our friends from the deep playing to the tune of the wind and rolling in its glory. They always came when we sat on those rocks, in twos and threes, arching through the water, sharing with us their sense of fun. As I watched the dolphins I became a part of their world, my world. But it was getting late.

'Time we went home, Maggs,' I said, holding her hand.

As the days passed, the sea enticed me like a spell. I would watch the surfers glide magi-

cally on the crest of amazing tunnels of water:
so peaceful, so alone, yet as one with all. I
remembered what Chris had said: they were
"finding their soul". He was young and yet he
talked like Aunty and understood connection.
I had to try and find this soul myself.

'How are you going, Edie?' said a distant
voice. It was Chris, joining me on my precious
rock. He'd remembered my name, and my
heart started to jump inside my chest. I felt
nervous at seeing him, but I liked the feeling.
He sat and told me of his adventures up and
down the coast, of his folks not understanding
him, of his friends and how they came to know
each other.

'We can talk without words,' he said. I knew
this because that's how Maggie and I would
talk. 'I have the same friendship with the sea.
We just know,' he said staring out as the dolphins lined the shore. 'How is your friend? Has
she cooled down?'

I explained the story of Rod to him, but felt
comfortable doing it. The sun was setting and
I realised it was time to go. 'Will you be here
tomorrow?' I asked.

'Yes, we'll be here. Bring Maggie along. I'll teach you to surf,' he said with a cheeky grin on his face.

'Okay,' I said and headed home.

After much persuading Maggs came, and what fun we had! We learnt to surf. We swam, we laughed and shared stories around a campfire on the beach at dusk, and we watched Chris and his friends glide across the moon. Chris's mate John warmed Maggie's heart, even though she was a lot younger than him. They walked along the shore and collected shells and each one listened as the other whispered stories.

Summer was closing and the spirit of the sun slowly fading, and when finally it was time to leave, a sadness that came from this new friendship drifted over us all.

'Girls, I've got something for you both,' Chris said, handing us each a single shelled leather necklace.

'Thank you,' we said in sequence.

Hugs and kisses were shared, and as they left Chris yelled, 'Hey, Edie!' He held onto his shell necklace. 'This is my soul.' They smiled and were gone.

Maggie knew at last that Rod's spirit was free and that no matter where he was, he was safe and that she had him—there in her hand.

A WARM, GENTLE BREEZE

Across the field I could see him, walking with his own special stride, waving, waving at me. The man with the dark hair and beard. He wasn't tall—he was quite short—but you could feel his presence, and his strength was obvious when the tall grass seemed to part as if it knew that it had to let him through.

Once again I woke suddenly. *That dream,* I thought. *I always have the same dream.* Who was this man? As I sank into the hollow of the bed, I wondered, and within minutes I could smell that fragrance. It was only subtle, but there it was once again. 'Every time I have that dream,' I mumbled under my breath, and it was gone. As quickly as I smelt it, it went! *Oh never mind,* I thought, *the answer will come one day.* It always did; I just had to be patient.

Aunty Gwen was busy darning old socks and doing a thousand other things. 'There's never enough hours in the day,' she said as I ventured happily into the kitchen, ready for my first day of work in the "real world", as Pop called it. I never quite knew what he was going on about. It was all the same world to me.

'Now, Edie, you know Mr Parsons likes you to wear a dress when you're serving folks. So go and change now. It's all part of what's proper,' Aunty said.

'Why? I like these jeans. They're ironed and it took me ages to get the crease just right,' I moaned.

'Edie!' she said in that bossy tone of hers. I couldn't win: one minute I was venturing out into the "real world" for my first part-time weekend job and the next I had to wear a "proper" dress. What was I? A child or a young adult? I seemed to be caught between the two, like a rocket shooting between Earth and Mars. Where was I?

I changed, just to make Uncle and Aunty happy.

'Now that's a girl, beautiful. You've got money in your hanky, and Pop will pick you up at 3 o'clock. Now have a good day and remember to be polite and use your manners,' Aunty said, smiling as she waved me goodbye.

Mr Parsons' shop was in the centre of town, and it was market day, so every man and his dog was about. Pop rang the bike bell and winked as I stepped off onto the kerb. Shame on him. I hated him ringing that silly bike bell: it was bad enough that I had to be doubled on his bike into town because we couldn't afford a car. How embarrassing! As I approached the shop my stomach twisted, I felt sick and, not watching where I was going, I tripped on the uneven concrete and down I went, clumsy, clumsy, clumsy.

'Are you all right?' I heard a soft voice, and as I looked up I recognised the face of a girl from school. But I couldn't place her.

'I'm fine, thanks,' I whispered.

'Edie, I thought it was you. How are you?' she said.

'Good. First day jitters!' I rolled my eyes.

'Me too. Are you working at Parso's shop?' she asked with excitement in her voice.

'Yeah.' Damn it, who was she? Two steps into the shop and Parso was there. Boy, was he a big man, and as he told us what to do, I smelt that fragrance, just a whiff and it was gone.

'It's a man's aftershave,' I blurted out loud and everyone looked at me.

'Pardon, Edie? You said something?' Mr Parsons asked.

'Oh no, sorry. Just talking to myself,' I said.

'If you need me, I'm out the back,' he said as he strolled to the kitchen.

We worked, we served, we smiled, I was very polite. We worked, we served, we smiled, I was very tired! Thank heavens for lunch! Mr Parsons encouraged us to go and sit in the park and eat our sandwiches.

'What a good idea,' I said, smiling softly at him. As we sat down to eat I said, 'Pop was right: this is the "real world".' I hesitated, 'I hope you don't think I'm rude, but I've forgotten your name.'

'Lisa. I was in cooking class with you, remember? I hated cooking class.' She sighed and continued, 'Yeah, my dad always said that to get anywhere in this world you have to work hard and give it your best shot.'

I couldn't have agreed more, but was money worth all this hard work? We chatted about studying and about her new school across the river and what we would do when we left. We had a lovely time. And it was funny that I'd never really got to know her at school. She could have been one of my best friends because we just hit it off straight away. There was something familiar about her as if I'd known her before.

Time went by and work called. This was one of many Saturdays that we spent sitting on a park bench exchanging stories and moments of laughter.

Trying to keep up with school work and working too was becoming quite a chore. I didn't seem to have time to do the things I liked most. Pop said it was giving me good grounding and character. It was giving me sore feet, I reckoned! Lisa and I became firm friends, and eventually we would walk to work together, chatting, chatting, chatting: we always had heaps to say.

We found we had something very much in common: both of us had lost a parent. Her dad had passed on only six months before and I'd lost my mum—well, I never really knew her, but I'd lost her. It's funny how you feel when someone walks in the same shoes.

A gentle breeze brushed across her face and she smiled. The sun was sending bright beams of gold to touch her hair with light and make her warm.

The dreams of the man waving stopped that day, for I knew he was truly happy. He had come to have me share friendship with his daughter and let her know that this was the "real world", and his strength and presence were within her.

And as Aunty said to me, 'From the earth we came, to the earth we return, and this is ours. And from this, God's greatest gifts to us are of love and friendship.'

To you, Lisa, with love...

DANCING
DOLPHINS

The moon had a mystery about her as she sat still in the night sky, watching us patiently, quietly waiting as we passed her by. As I sat and admired her beauty under the willow tree, the silence of the night air was disrupted by the soft ripples beneath my toes.

My line was moving ever so subtly. *I've got one!* I thought, looking up.

'Thanks, Uncle Billy,' I said softly. Uncle Billy was an old fisherman from way back and he taught me to be a fish, so to speak, by attaching a fishing line and hook onto my toe.

He said I could feel them as they passed downstream.

'The moon is their mother and she guides them. They have a special meeting place,' he would say to Pop often, when he was passing through for a quick visit. I sat for hours listening to his yarns. I thought he had a wonderful life: no troubles, just him and the road.

He lives beneath the water now, swimming free and rolling among the waves. Aunty misses her brother the most and she doesn't like me to talk about him.

'The old buzzard!' she says. 'Leaving those children to walk alone.' That's it: nothing more; nothing less.

Yes, I've got one! A beauty, small and silvery, nicely baked with heaps of golden sunshine on top. Yum! I thought.

You had to be very quiet, though. The silly things thought they were caught in a breeze. I could just scoop him out with my faithful net, no worries. Then it was time to go home. Holidays were great: no school, no homework, no thinking!

Time slips away when you are having fun. I

often met Maggie under the old willow but this day she couldn't make it. She had kin coming, Uncle Stan's pack. Dusted moonbeams guided me on my path home. Aunty was going to be pleased with my catch because it would be enough for a good feed.

'Who says girls can't catch fish, Troy?' I yelled into the night sky, as I flung my tinny over the back fence. Hoping he would hear me, the boy who fumbled over his own feet whenever he came near me. It was funny the way he was always big mouthing himself around us girls, then tripping over his own words.

'Good. You're home, Edie. Did you catch many?' Aunty asked.

'Yes, enough for all of us,' I said proudly, holding my tinny up for her to see.

'Can you make it stretch, Gwen?' Pop asked.

I was puzzled. 'There's plenty! I'll get some wood'. And as I raced outside, I noticed someone standing in the shadows of the verandah. 'Oh geez, who's there?' I screeched, my heart doing flips.

The door opened and Pop almost jumped

out. 'Don't worry, love. It's your cousin,' he said gently, lending a soothing hand to me and reassuring the girl I could see now standing nervously in the shadows.

Then Aunty stepped out. 'Edie, this is your cousin Angie.' I stood there amazed. It was like looking at myself in the mirror. And it seemed like neither of us moved forever.

We sat down to eat but not a word was spoken. Where did this shy image of myself come from—and why? I hadn't met her before, didn't even know she existed. No one had ever spoken of her. *Oh well*, I thought, *she was here now.*

It was the holidays and there was another girl to join our gang. Great! Or so I thought.

As the sun brightened up our lives, days would run into each other, as if they were racing to get me back to school. Angie and I became sort of friends. I did all the talking and she did all the listening. But Maggie thought she was deaf.

'Maybe we could sign to her,' she said quietly.

'Don't be stupid! She can talk. She just

don't want to,' I said, making another superb footy pass to Maggs. I could outrun the boys, and always scored the most goals. Our mixed team had won the touch footy round the summer before.

'But I only wish those boys wouldn't fall all over me,' I whinged to Elizabeth.

'You'll just have to keep up your speed, Edie,' she said as we scored another goal. As I walked off the field, I caught Angie talking to herself. Oh no, she wasn't deaf, she was mad! I needed to listen, so I watched her.

As we strolled home, not a word was said. 'Angie, you're awfully quiet today. Did you like my last run? We got them good and hard today and...'

'You run like an emu, bub,' she interrupted me. Her words were light and breezy, so light they passed you by and sometimes you wouldn't even understand what she was blabbing about.

'Uummm, why don't you come for a run next week?' I asked. I wanted to see her form. She probably ran like an elephant. Maggie thought Angie was annoying, so she left me with her. Great friend!

Aunty said that I had to be kind because Angie was lonely. Well, I was starting to get lonely with all her conversation. It was like talking to my fish!

Jimmy, Roger, Dawn and Bob were visiting, so I felt better because I didn't have to do all the talking. These old people had a way. If Rog brought the didg, there would be aching happy feet beside the fire.

Jimmy's yarns were famous for bringing folks in from all over the place. Bob would disappear, and the howling noises would begin. Jimmy's stories would hold you as if he'd placed a spell on you. And he'd change his voice, so you didn't quite know if it was him or the men upstairs.

As the moon slowly rose and joined our story, creepy, rustling sounds loitered around us. 'Which animal is that?' I whispered, scaring myself and hopefully Angie. She huddled in close to the fire, scared out of her brain!

I kept watching her. What was racing through her mind? She hardly said a word, and we seemed to be growing more distant as the holiday went by. There was no possible way she was related to me; she didn't talk enough.

The next morning I decided I would be more Christian. Aunty would say, 'Remember we are all made the same, Edie. The same blood running through our veins supplying life to the same organs. We've just got different coverings and different ways of being.' These words were ringing in my mind. As I raced into the sitting room, Aunty reminded me that today was Angie's birthday and I had to be kind to her.

Our home only had two bedrooms, so that's where guests always slept. 'Hey, Angie! Wake up! Let's go down the beach!' I yelled, flinging back the bedcovers. But she wasn't there! I could still feel her body heat from the mattress, so she hadn't gone too far.

I really lived in God's country. From the peak of the hill you could see over the trees and smell the salt. At times if you were still enough, you could feel the sea's mist touching you gently.

I scanned the horizon, trying to see Angie.

Then I heard that familiar whistling sound brush my ears. 'Maggs! Glad you came. I'm searching for Angie. She's gone walkabout.'

Maggie rolled her eyes. 'Don't bother finding her. She's weird. Let's go down the beach.'

'No, we have to try this one last time to be her friend. She's not like us, but we have to get to know her if only for Aunty's sake,' I said, as I raced her through the clover.

'We don't have to be nice to everyone,' she grumbled under her breath. We ran and ran until we came to the shore, both of us looking up and down her golden edge. The beach was really busy at this time of the day and we couldn't see Angie anywhere.

'Maggs, let's sit and try and feel out which way she headed,' I said, puffing.

'Oh—use our gut feeling? All right then,' Maggie hesitated. 'My gut feeling tells me that I need to head tooooooo—the shop! I'm starved!' Leaping to her feet, she turned and said, 'Aren't you coming?'

'No, just wait,' I said abruptly. I pointed in the direction of the cove and what seemed a minute after that, Troy and his mates raced by.

'You looking for Angie? She's at the cove, and I mean at the very edge of the cove. She's lost it, and I think she's going to jump. I'm getting dad!' Troy yelled. His dad was one of the policemen in town. Within a moment we were there, and there was Angie, just sitting on the very edge of the cliff and staring out to sea

'Now, Edie, we'll walk slowly so as not to scare her. Just try and get her attention,' Maggs muttered. I'm sure she could hear my heart pounding and she turned back and waved to her.

'Nice day, Angie! Great one for a swim. Do you want to come down the beach with us?' I yelled against the wind. We kept gaining ground.

'No, not yet. I need to watch,' she said.

Both Maggs and I exchanged a glance. 'Watch what?' we said, puzzled.

'They will be here soon!' she said. Under my breath I told Maggs that I thought she wouldn't jump.

'How do you know?' she said.

'Because this is the most she's ever spoken

48

to me. Something's going on. Let's join her!' So we did. We were very high up and we were frightened.

Heights aren't my favourite thing. But I knew I had to be with her.

We all sat in silence. Then from over the ridge we could hear footsteps pounding the earth. Troy had kept his word. How was I going to explain this one to Pop? The worst was that I didn't think I could get up from this spot. I could feel the breeze slipping through the backs of my knees, my legs dangling in mid-air. Were we too heavy and the earth—could it hold us? Maybe it would give way, and I would die a horrible death splattered on the rocks for the sharks to feast off my skinny carcass.

I started to panic. 'I have to go, I have to go, I have to go,' I said, panting. Maggie held my hand. She realised the situation that Angie had got us into.

Calmly she said, 'Angie, let's go. I think Edie's feeling sick.'

Angie just looked at us and said, 'No.' The

police arrived and a small party of people followed.

Troy yelled out, 'Edie, you all right?' I couldn't answer, and Maggie just waved. From behind us Constable Higgins asked if we needed help to get up. He asked us to wave if we did. The silence was deadly.

Angie spoke, 'Edie, please give me a minute. They're coming. I can feel them. They're coming!'

Time stood still, the breeze dropped and then the most amazing thing happened. The sun changed its shade from that of a golden yellow to a soft mauve colour and there on the edge of the world danced twenty, thirty or even forty dolphins. They came from nowhere, and as the sun finished its display, the dancing dolphins disappeared.

Everyone who saw this wonderful scene believed it truly to be a miracle.

A gift, I realised later, from Uncle Billy, Angie's father, who died suddenly of a heart attack as he hauled in his fishing boat after a day's fishing. A special gift for her fifteenth birthday with the promise that he would always watch over her.

Uncle Billy's yarns were famous for bringing folks back home. And on this day Angie, Maggie, myself and all those who shared this extraordinary experience became aware that the special meeting place wasn't far away: it lives within us as we journey. We just have to believe.

LOST SHOES

Sifting through the black and white photos, I saw him again, that boy. He looked familiar but who was he? My mind gave me flashes of mud slinging and pie making and bright pearly teeth in a grin that warmed the heart. But who was he? I just sat staring and trying to remember.

'Have you got my slippers?' yelled Aunty. My heart skipped a beat and I was off dreaming and looking at things that Aunty said held sacred memories of a time of joy and love that the mind, when it becomes old, can sometimes forget.

I fumbled, 'I'm coming!' and pushed the

black and white photos into an old biscuit tin that was already too small.

'Edie, you're nosing when I told you not to,' Aunty said, towering over me. She didn't look too impressed.

'Oh sorry, Aunty. I couldn't find one of the slippers, and, well, I knocked the tin accidentally and all the photos fell out and...'

'Now settle down. Here it is, right beside my other slipper,' she said, peering at me under arched eyebrows. 'Lying, Edie, only plays havoc with your mind. Now go and sit by the fire and let me dry that hair of yours.' I knew she wasn't mad, but I did know that there was a time and place to discuss matters of the heart with Aunty, usually when she was singing or humming at the world and she would quietly share stories. And Pop would smile as he listened. They would occasionally exchange a funny sort of look because they were talking without words, just like Maggs and me. They were good friends.

I sat in my nightie in front of the fire. Our home was not much but it was warm and not because of the fire, because it just was. I settled comfortably in front of Aunty, and I could feel the gentle firmness of her hand as it brushed my hair into order again and she started to hum sweetly. Once more she was lost in thought. Thinking back to that photo, I really needed to know who that boy was!

'Aunty, in the tin there is a picture of a boy,' I whispered.

'The one you were holding?' she asked.

'Yes, who is he? I feel like I know him,' I said.

After what seemed like ages, she said softly, 'That is Toby, Old Sam's grandson.' My mind wasn't playing tricks, now I knew why I had flashes of mud slinging and mud pies. We used to go down the creek and make the most awful mess with the cloudy water as it gathered bits of the earth in its rush to reach the waterfall. Toby would always tease me but I didn't mind really. It was all in fun, but I had to get the last word, so we'd end up throwing mud at each other. The last time I can remember, I got him a beauty: splat, right in the middle of his head! He couldn't even see me as I went running home. I'd won, again!

'I don't remember him like that. He looked

different. And why has he got those boots hanging around his head?' I asked with a frown. Silence is deadly, and I knew I was going to hear something that would leave me with that empty feeling in my gut again. This time Aunty just sat and looked at Pop.

He said, 'Edie, let me tell you a story of some lost shoes.

'Toby was fifteen years old when that photo was taken. It was taken, let's just say, a long way from here. Remember the black shiny cars? Well, they go to many other homes, and one day they went to Old Sam's farm, unexpected might I add, only some folks knew that Toby lived with Old Sam. Anyway, this day they came, Toby was escorted gently into the car by the fancy-dressed men, and they drove off with him. Where to, Old Sam didn't even know.

'Over time Old Sam was allowed to see him, and during one rare visit he was given that photo you're asking about. Toby apparently worked for some folks who owned a mill. He would walk two miles every day to that mill. And the mill folk gave him only the one pair of shoes to wear. They were too big. He told his grandfather that the shoes didn't fit him, so because he loved to walk with no shoes on anyway, and feel the earth under his toes, he decided he'd hang them around his neck until they fitted him properly.

'As the story goes, Old Sam took the shoes home, concealing them inside his jacket. He promised Toby he'd fix them for him and when he was allowed to come home for a visit they'd be a perfect fit.'

'What did he do with them, Pop?' I asked.

'Well, love, Old Sam polished and repaired them and hung them on the front verandah, new leather laces tied securely together awaiting his return. They hung, waiting and waiting...' Pop's voice drifted away in thought.

Aunty continued the story and spoke over Pop's soft whisper. 'Edie, those shoes have been hanging there now for five years, waiting for Toby to come home. Because you see,' she paused, 'they'll fit him now!'

Toby never saw Old Sam again. He passed away years later, and you know, those shoes are still hanging on that verandah.

We all walk many roads in our lives; some

directions are easier than others, and some paths never come to an end.

I wonder where he is now.

BLACK
COCKATOOS

Lush ferns and soft moonlight. The circle is forming, the cries are heard, commanding all to attend. You can hear their call, but it is not so much heard. It is felt, it is needed. It is time.

Aunty Gwen always passed a sense of mystery to anyone who listened to her words. Sometimes they were simple but other times they left you not really understanding at all. Her knowledge lay in the mystery of the unspoken feelings you were left with and that you would share with someone else. So the day when this particular sharing came, it was between myself and Matty.

'Edie, get ready. The Good Lord needs you to be your best today,' Aunty said, humming an old churchy hymn.

'I'm coming,' I hollered back. I hated dressing up to go to church. Did God really care that I wasn't all scrubbed up? We walked along the dusty road, at a slow pace that suited the old folk. Pop's shoes reflecting the sunshine, it seemed the dust didn't dare lay its film over them.

'Hurry up, Edie,' I could hear him saying. 'Your dreaming is slowing us down, love.'

'Okay, but tell me, Pop, why must we go every Sunday to church? Don't you say that God is everywhere? Why can't I just sit under the old oak? God'll listen!' I exclaimed.

Pop's silence was deadly but Aunty spoke up, 'You're right: the earth is our Mother, and like all mothers who nurture our young within our womb—a space where darkness, light and love become one—the earth gives us a gift for all to share and grow from. But it starts within. Church is the praising from within. Remember that.' And with that, her strides became longer. I followed, thinking about her words, and hardly realised we were already stepping onto the polished wooden floorboards of the old church on the hill.

I always thought it smelt holy, and the holy water smelt that way too. The water even tasted strange! We would always sit up the front, nodding as we passed the many familiar faces; Jimmy Dell's foot slipping out from under the pew, as he eyed me cheekily. He missed again. I thought, *He must think I'm stupid or something.*

Maggs and her family never missed a Sunday either. We were both doomed to do this forever.

The sermon started and like a parrot I recited every word. *Why couldn't a lady say the same words,* I thought. Anyway, it was over before I knew it and Maggs and I got to take off our shoes and socks and paddle in the puddles left on the sides of the road after the long rains. We left the older folks straggling behind.

As we got near the fork in the road, we said our goodbyes and headed home for Sunday lunch. Now this was the best part of Sunday! Food! Uncle Cyril was waiting on the verandah and we hadn't seen him for such a long time. He was Aunty's brother. You know, I got questioned about my light skin, but I knew who I was. Uncle Cyril, well he must have had such a hard time: folks always staring because he was half black and half white.

'Colour is only skin deep,' I remembered Pop saying. Uncle Cyril had brought a visitor, young Matty my cousin, and as we welcomed them into the house, Matty and I ran off to the tree house.

'Change those clothes, Edie. You'll get them dirty,' yelled Aunty over the distant chugging of Old Sam's tractor. So I ran back and changed.

The tree house was a great hideout, and whenever Matty came, he settled in there like a brown snake hibernating. He never spoke much, but he would gather some thick sticks and always managed to have string in his pockets to tie them up and make lookouts. We had lookouts everywhere.

'Watch out, Edie! They're coming. Hear their call overhead? Duck!' he screamed.

'Who? Who's coming?' I asked.

'The black cockatoos.'

'So what? They're always flying around here; they're just coming to say hello,' I said bewildered. And with that he jumped to the floor of the cubby and cowered into a bushy corner. He was shaking, so I jumped down and tried to comfort him.

'Don't worry, Matty. I'll look after you. No birds are going to hurt my cousin!' I said bravely. Why was he so scared? I wondered. It was my job to look after him, though.

The day slipped by and I knew when it was time to leave because I could smell our lunch!

Lunch as usual was delicious, and it filled us right up to the brim. Aunty always put on a nice spread. Uncle Cyril sat quietly throughout the meal and soon my favourite chair was calling, so we moved to the verandah. Matty sat at Uncle Cyril's feet and rested his blond mop against his knees. What was wrong? The afternoon sun curled its rays gently around us, warming and comforting. Aunty called out to Matty to come and help her with something. This was her time to talk to him, I knew. She'd talk to you while she was cleaning. I thought she was quite clever because that's how she got me to do so many chores around the place.

Now was my time to ask Uncle Cyril what was wrong with Matty and why those birds scared him so much.

'Give him time, give him time. Young Matty fears they are calling him to take him to their sacred circle. You see, Edie, they weren't always black. Long, long ago, they were like me: their coverings were majestic; they had white crests and black bodies. They would fill the blue sky with their beauty, their sweet singing voices alerting all to their presence. And announcing that all was good with the earth. There were many of them.

'One day a woman came. Her heart was bleeding and her mind wove thoughts like cobwebs. The love she had within had died, her children were gone, and the earth was bad. She heard the cockatoos rejoicing and their singing burned her. Her anger at such happiness grasped her soul, so she started to throw rocks at them, and they fell from the sky. And with her tangled mind, she gathered them and made a fire and placed their carcasses in the coals. As the other cockatoos looked on, they cried sweetly for their brothers and sisters.

'The woman's loss hurt those special creatures and from that day on, the cockatoos hid from peering, painful eyes, disguising themselves in black for fear of showing their beauty. The loss of their brothers and sisters makes them rare and mysterious. Their voices cry for the echoing pain of those who are gone. The earth is their Mother; they love her and they gather still today to give praise, privately, crying across the skies as they give thanks in circles beneath on the bush's gentle fern floor.'

I dared not ask what this had to do with Matty. Uncle Cyril's story left me thinking, which my people's stories always do. As the sun steadily heated the verandah, Aunty came out with Matty, her arm around him lovingly.

Uncle Cyril left, but this time without Matty, so I had a new member of my family: Matty had come to live with us. His mother had many children, but she didn't want him. He wasn't right, she told Uncle: he was too white. The love she had for him in her womb got tangled up in the cobwebs of her mind. But that love is eternal. Sadly, her pain couldn't cope with his difference. She told him the story of the black cockatoos, so her fear was fed to him. Now it was time for us to heal the wounds.

The circle is forming, the cries are heard commanding all to attend. Listen... You can hear their call, but it is not so much heard; it is felt, it is needed, it is time.

Welcome to our family, little brother.

THE RAINMAKER

The sky opened up a fierce attack on her sister the earth. Finally, after what seemed months, the rains came! Cold to the touch, refreshing to feel. And they affected everyone.

Folks in town were always talking about their crops and their tanks. Even Maggie and I would talk about the rain, although we had the beach to soothe our souls. You see, the rain meant fresh vegies, being able to have longer showers and having them more often. Everything had more life about it, even the people.

Touching the cold window now with the rain

streaming down outside, I could see Old Dora in my mind. Dora was Old Sam's sister. Many townsfolk thought she was strange. Some said she was an old black witch, but as Maggie would say, what's colour got to do with it? I reckoned that her magic was what you let it be. Some things I knew; others, I just had to believe.

'Edie, buckets!' hollered Aunty and I bounced off my bed, knowing exactly what I had to do. You see, Pop was a bit too old to fix the leaky roof. Aunty said those holes had been there since he was knee-high to a grasshopper, so tins and buckets of all shapes and sizes decorated our home. Over the years, the rains had grown many tins!

It was nice to feel the crisp, cold tingle that the rain brings. It's funny how you can smell her approaching. And it really did put a spring in your step. Wasn't long and all my chores were done, so it was time to ring Maggs.

'Aunty, can Maggs stay over this weekend? Please, Aunty. I'll still do my work,' I said.

'Slow down, Edie! Yes she can stay and, don't worry, you've worked really hard around here without my continually asking. Now out with you! Go and enjoy the rain,' she said. Gee, I was lucky. I didn't have a mum or dad around, but Aunty and Pop always made my heart sing.

A quick call and Maggs was meeting me down the creek at Grey Gum corner.

Running through the rain, holding my old boots tightly in my hands, with each splash making rings around my muddy toes. The rain found its way down through every fibre I was wearing. Rain, glorious rain!

Maggie was waiting patiently, her pack protecting her head. She didn't like the rain as much as I did.

'How's it going?' I shouted above the noise on the tin roof of our hideout.

'Great! Got my pack and the stone.' She had a twinkle in her eye. We had plans this weekend. Talk was flying from one end of town to the other. Old Dora was casting spells. Some reported that they'd heard her saying she was going to turn those whites into blacks because they were sapping the very soul of this land.

You know, the black shiny car would still

come to our house, but they never did get me because I was as sly as a lizard camouflaged by the scrub. Aunty said Old Dora was harmless and she just had a bad temper.

'Is it any wonder?' I would often hear her saying to Pop.

So Maggs and I were taking our stones to Old Dora. She said they could give us wisdom and she would show us how. We didn't care what those folks in town thought: she was Old Sam's sister!

We walked back home slowly and talked about our plan to get to Old Dora's without Aunty and Pop finding out. We'd have to go at dusk. 'We have to tell a white lie, Edie,' said Maggie.

'What?' I asked.

'Well, we could say that we are going to bed early, because we want to go to the beach to see the dancing dolphins.'

'No, Maggs. Pop sneaks in a couple of times every night and checks me and the windows, so that's no good. How about we tell them we need to go to your house to get your boots?' I said.

'No,' Maggie sighed. 'Aunty would call my mum to see if we'd arrived safely.'

But we just had to go! This was very important.

When we were nearly home, we realised our luck was in. We could hear Daph, one of Aunty's friends, talking really loudly on the verandah. Boy, could they yarn!

'Oh, can you believe it, Maggs? We must be meant to go. Listen, Daph's here visiting. She's talking so loud, she musn't have her hearing aid turned up. They'll never hear us leave now,' I whispered.

'What about Pop?' Maggie asked.

'Oh, he'll be listening to the radio. There's a show on around 6 o'clock and it goes for an hour. That's all we have,' I said.

Plan in action, rain still streaming down, we were ready.

We had dinner and went to my room to read. Lazing back on my bed, Maggie asked, 'Do you think Old Dora can really change white folks into black fellas? Wouldn't that be funny!' she laughed.

'Don't know. She's tricky. Imagine it, Maggs.

Some folks would have to leave their big homes and come to our side of the creek. What's the big deal about colour anyway? Your skin's lighter than mine, but it doesn't mean we can't be friends.'

'No, I think we're special, hey, Edie,' Maggie said, staring out the window.

I said, 'No, we're just not stupid.' And we looked at each other.

The time was right. Daphne and Aunty were still yarning and Pop was tuning in his radio, so out my window and we were off, our feet moving faster than time. Old Dora's light was on so we sneaked up and, peering through the window, we could see her. She was humming a tune we didn't know and over on a table, a pile of stones sat listening.

'You tap,' Maggie indicated to me, so I did.

'Come in, girls,' called Old Dora.

'How did she know it was us?' I whispered to Maggs. Just then shivers started rolling up and down my spine. We opened the door and went in.

'Thought it was you,' she said, smiling. We sat down and just watched her for what seemed like ages. She never had very much to say but her presence spoke a louder conversation. 'Now, girls, have you your stones and did you tell your folks you were coming here?' she asked.

'Oh, yes!' blurted out Maggie. Butter wouldn't melt in her mouth sometimes.

'Okay, then come with me.' And she headed towards the back door, and outside another heap of stones sat all in exact order on top of each other, forming a pyramid. My heart started to beat like a train on a track. What was she going to do? Would we ever see our folks again? And worse still, I thought, she might turn me into a white fella! My mind was beside itself.

Silence. Rain touched the stillness of the air but I couldn't hold my tongue. 'Dora, you aren't going to turn me white and Maggs dark, are you?' Words poured out of my mouth like sap trickling from an old wattle tree.

Surprised, she just looked at me. 'What do you mean? I can't change the colour of folks. They do that themselves,' she said.

Maggie looked angrily at me. 'Geez, Edie.'

Then she explained, 'Dora, folks been talking in town and we just thought with your stones and all...'

'Girls, sit and listen. There's no need to be afraid of me. Be afraid of the words of ignorant folks. They don't understand, so they make up stories in their minds to cover for their laziness in not trying to find the truth,' she said, staring sadly at the dark sky.

Time allowed us to settle with her thoughts.

'Edie, Maggie,' she said. 'Some folks in town only listen to what they want to hear. This makes their judgment of others easy. Yes, I do have a sacred space where I ask Mother Earth to cast her spell, but it's good—not bad.' Still talking, Old Dora moved slowly over to the pile of stones and solemnly placed them in a circle, with us in the centre. 'Anything is possible. You just have to believe. Ask Mother Earth for anything, but respect is important. This circle is my sacred space. The stones connect me to the earth, and help send my messages of goodness.' She paused for a minute, looking at the earth and the stones, and softly brushing the earth in a circular movement. Maggs and

I looked at each other and an eerie feeling filled the air. By now we were soaked to the bone. Maggie started to shiver, but it didn't matter: we had to finish.

'Girls, you know the earth has been so dry, affecting everyone's spirit, with the heat of the day and the sky lined with white trails. I knew after a while that we needed to see a change of colour, so I asked for the white to turn to black!' Dora said.

'CLOUDS!' yelled Maggie, her voice echoing above the noise of the rain. 'White clouds into black clouds. You brought the rain, Dora!'

'Yes!' Dora smiled.

'So with your sacred stones you asked for rain, not changing folks' colours,' I shouted loudly. 'Wow, that's amazing, I have to tell Aunty and Pop,' I said.

'No, Edie they know. Some folks just know that we all belong to the earth and each other. There's an understanding.'

Time passed and Old Dora showed us how our stones could give us wisdom. We both realised that she wasn't a witch but a very special person, who worked for the goodness of all in her own unique way. We said our good-byes and made it home without my folks realising we had gone.

And as for Old Dora, Maggie and I reckoned in a funny magical way, she had a direct line to God, because they could work wonders together.

THE LEGACY

Summer was approaching and the town was alive with excitement. It was Gala day. And many busy hands and fast-moving feet carried the message: "Your donations help our children". The money raised from the day would go to our school and we needed books badly.

'Those legacies aren't coming in as often now!' Aunty exclaimed, beating her cake mixture vigorously.

'What's a legacy, Aunty?' I asked.

'Well, love, old folks that pass on, they decide to give money to the school. They leave it in writing and then Mr Jones buys books for the children to read.' She smiled gently and kept beating, while my finger skimmed the edge of the bowl for a taste.

'Folks seem to be staying here longer these days, so it was decided that we needed a special day to raise money for our books.'

I just loved the smell of the oven turning the simple flour into little tasty delights and I sneaked one from under the tea towel.

'Edie!' I could hear Aunty as I slipped out quietly through the screen door. 'There'll be none left if you kids keep eating them,' I could hear her saying as a flash of golden locks sped past me.

'Hey, Matty, wait!' I yelled, racing to catch up to that cheeky grin.

'I got a handful, Edie. You weren't quick enough!' Matty was always trying to outrun me, but it was impossible. I won the running races every year at school.

'Let's go down the creek. I'll race you!' he said, already way ahead.

'That's not fair!' I yelled. 'You got a head start!' The creek wasn't far and I knew a shortcut, so within a wink it was on.

When I ran, nothing else mattered. Under the old rickety fence, past Tommo's creek, crossing the creek-bed rocks that Maggs and I put there—one, two, three, four, fi—! *Splash!* Water suddenly up to my pants. 'Oh, darn it!' Where was rock five? I belted the water with my fist. Who moved it?

On the breath of the breeze I could hear laughter. Matty thought this was real funny. 'Bet you, Edie: told you I was faster than you.' By now he was rolling around with laughter. 'You look stupid!' I could hear him proclaiming his glory for all to hear.

'Come and help me. I've gone over on my ankle again. Darn it, darn it, darn it! These silly ankles always take me down,' I yelled.

'Okay don't get your knickers in a knot,' he said as he held my arm.

'Maggs is already down at the creek. Real sad she is, I don't know what's wrong, though.'

We made our way there. Sprawled out on the soft velvet grass was Maggie, sad and all.

'What's up, Maggs?' I asked. Lately she was always in a sad mood, snapping at me, and I was just about fed up. It seemed we were fighting but we weren't, and I couldn't quite work it out. She wouldn't talk either, so I decided to just leave her alone.

'Nothing,' she mumbled under her breath.

'Want a biscuit?' Matty held out a crumbled handful.

'No thanks, Matt,' she said sombrely.

'What's eating you?' I asked.

'Oohh, geez. *Girl* talk,' interrupted Matty. 'I'm going skimming.' And off he went, looking for the flattest stones.

'What is it, Maggs? Lately you're always angry with me. What have I done? Tell me, are we fighting or not?' I blurted out impatiently. I could fight real well with Aunty and Pop, but with my friends, well, I didn't like to do that.

'All right, but you have to promise not to get mad with me,' she faltered over every word.

'I won't. I promise,' I said.

'Well, you know when we were trying out for the running races at school?'

'Yeah,' I said.

'Well, as we were walking back with the teachers and parents after the tryouts, I overheard two of the parents say that those light kids could never beat our kids, and that Maggie, meaning me, was no competition for the likes of Edie. Angela was with me and she said that we were being discrimm...or something against.'

'Discriminated, Maggie. Aunty told me what it means,' I said.

'Well, I got real mad. I was fuming. Who do they think they are! I can run fast, I know I can, because no one at school can catch me when we play. But what's worst is, is, that I told Lauren and Emma and—you know what big mouths they've got—well, it's all over school. I couldn't believe those parents said that about me.'

As I listened I started to fume too. My friend, my very best friend, was talking about me behind my back. 'Geez, thanks a lot, Maggie. I thought you were my friend. What's our skin got to do with the speed of our legs? Nothing—you know that,' I yelled at her, gulping in heaps of air. I got the hiccups, just as I always did when I was real angry. 'I'm going home. Thanks a lot!'

I could hear her voice, 'Please, Edie, I just

want to win sometimes. I didn't mean it. Please come back, *please.*'

When I walked in with a throbbing ankle and the hiccups, Pop knew something was wrong. 'Love, sit down and show me that swollen spud,' he said in his usual gentle way. 'Now what have you been doing? Matty came back a long time ago, so where have you been to get this?' He placed moist cabbage leaves lightly over the swelling.

'Nothing, Pop. I just missed a rock in the creek bed, that's all.' I didn't like to tell him too much because he worried so much about me and he was old.

'Why are you so angry, love? You know you can't pull the wool over my eyes. Your hiccups are a dead give-away,' he said, prompting me.

'It's nothing. Only, well, Maggs and I had a little fight, that's all,' I said, arching back in the chair as the pain pulsed its anger through me.

'Edie, love, friendship is a gift. We are all different but it's working through that differ-ence that makes the gift rewarding. Do you understand?' he said, rubbing my leg.

'Yes, I do.' I was really more concerned with my pain than his words.

'Are you all ready? Edie, where have you been? Oh dear, we were just about to leave for town. The biscuits are all ready to go. What happened? Those ankles of yours don't seem to have much strength,' Aunty said briskly.

'I'll stay and keep an eye on her. You take Matty and help raise the money for the school,' Pop said.

'No, no, no,' she said.

'Gwen, no one sells your biscuits as fine as you do. The school's in desperate need of those books, so go. Everything will be fine here. You'll be okay, Edie, won't you?' Pop's glasses slipped slightly down his nose as he looked at me to reassure her.

'I'm all right, Aunty, I am,' I rolled my eyes.

With a little huff she proceeded to leave. 'Rest, and keep it up, okay?' The school was in good hands.

The afternoon sun warmed me as I lay thinking about what Maggs had done. Why did she have to tell everyone? Who cared what those parents had said and why should it have mattered who wins? My stomach was twisted with wondering what to do. Maybe I could tell Pop, but he was going to be really annoyed that folks were causing such trouble. Worse still was that those big-mouthed girls would love to get others against me and they'd start a war!

Pop ventured out onto the verandah and sat in his comfortable chair. 'Aahh, what a nice summer's day,' he said, gently rocking himself. As I watched him, my thoughts were urging me to tell him about my dilemma. The battle was on, but this time it was in my own mind. I didn't fight with Maggs very often, and it hurt. The old folk had a knowing, didn't they? Pop started talking about the old days when he could outrun his father's horse and cart and somehow, I don't know how, I shared my woes with him.

'The Gala Day was a success, and thanks to all your parents we are able to purchase many new books for you to read.' Mr Jones's words echoed around the Monday-morning assembly. School was always there, but hobbling around wasn't my way of enjoying it. Maggie didn't go to school that week. Her mum told Aunty she had an upset stomach, but I knew she was feeling guilty and didn't want to face me.

During that whole week the air at school was uneasy. Lauren and her friends were ignoring me and I could hear whispering whenever I got near them.

'You think you're better than us, don't you, Edie? Your kind are shameful,' they teased. This was really getting me down. Tryouts continued for our carnival and my ankle was increasing in strength, but my spirit wasn't. What could I do? How could you change words already spoken?

Aunty was called up to the school because Matty had been involved in fights, and he was being accused of causing the tension around the place.

'I'm sorry, but Matty is cussing and upsetting children with his remarks,' Mr Jones told Aunty. 'This can't go on. We have a school where all are treated equal, so you must talk to him now, or I have no alternative but to ask him to leave.' His voice sounded harsh as I overheard Aunty repeat his words to Pop. Even at home, a darkness fell. Matty wouldn't talk to me about it, but I knew. I knew it was because of the talk that Maggie had started!

We were divided and the feeling was just like having butterflies in your stomach constantly. They never went away, they wouldn't settle and their restless movements were a reminder that all wasn't well. The next week Maggie came back to school and we hadn't talked all that time. My special friendship was broken, a smashed mirror with pieces that didn't reflect a complete picture anymore.

The carnival was the following Wednesday. Mr Jones took our class for a special treat, as he often did, usually when there was some message to be shared. We gathered at the back of the schoolyard, and as we slipped under the fence, we took our usual track into the bush to the clearing where, years before, he'd built us a campfire site. This day he'd asked us to bring in sausages. We cooked them and sat and enjoyed the taste. But we didn't sit for long before he asked us to follow him, and off we went on a small bushwalk.

As we ventured along the path, Jordan

stopped. 'Hey, Mr Jones, can I get some?' He pointed to the sap oozing out of the old gum.

'Yes, looks sweet, Jordie,' he replied. Mr Jones stopped and watched the sap, and we wondered what he was doing. 'You know, the sap is liquid gold given to you from the tree, a food to savour and to bring life to your taste-buds. It can come in all colours, but that doesn't matter: its goodness is always the same.' And he went on with the walk, leaving us to think about what he'd said.

Then it was Wednesday, sports carnival day, and the bright morning smiled as I entered the kitchen. I was ready, I'd show them; my ankle was well again. I grabbed a chair and waited as Aunty poured me a bowl of porridge. Pop and Matty joined us.

'Well, you kids have a nice sunny day for your carnival. Pop and I will be there to cheer you on,' she said, sprinkling too much sugar on her porridge.

'Hope I do well today. I'm a bit nervous,' I said, tying back my hair.

'Have you and Maggie made up?' Pop asked. 'It's about time you sorted out your differences.'

'Hmm,' I said.

'It's only what you make of it, Edie,' Aunty remarked. 'Now off you go and have fun.'

As we said our goodbyes, Aunty yelled out, 'Remember, Edie. Go and be proud. You can make the difference!' And with that, she closed the door.

There was so much activity at school with everyone preparing for their race, I didn't take much notice of anyone else because I had to concentrate if I was going to win. It was time for our race: Maggie and I were in the same one, but we didn't wish each other good luck, like we used to. Mr Jones came with Father Mac and because he was the priest, he had the honour of starting the races. A nice old man, holy he was.

'On your mark, get set, GO!'

We were off, sprinting like rabbits out of their burrows. As I looked ahead I realised I was in front. I'd left the others behind. Then as I looked, the blonde strands of Maggie's hair were flickering in the wind, right beside me. *Oh no*, I thought, *I have to win*. She overtook me and the finishing line was just ahead. The cheers from the crowd spurred me on. It was in sight, one last push, and I just had to do it. Suddenly, there was the pain again, my blasted ankle, and over I went.

'No, no!' I groaned, as I looked up and I could feel arms lifting me to my feet.

It was Maggie! 'Come on, Edie. We're doing this together.' And with one swift movement, we walked over the finishing line arm in arm, and the other kids in our race walked over too. The crowd's loud clapping said it all. We won, we all did.

Mr Jones's message had got through.

OUTSIDE THE DOGTAG

An owl hooted and there was a solitary figure in the darkness. Slithering like a snake about to attack its prey, we watched as Old Pete sat there. He was a lonely, wandering soul and Matty and I knew that he'd be down by the creek. The hooting owl had guided us to him.

Old Pete was one of Pop's wartime buddies and sometimes he would venture into town and pay Pop a visit but he never stayed long, and all Pop's hospitality didn't persuade him to spread out his swag.

Their talks were quiet as they remembered the days gone by, and when Old Pete left he would give Matty, not me, a simple pencil drawing. And that annoyed me. Matty had kept them all.

'Another one!' I exclaimed as I grabbed it from his hands. 'Let's pin it up like the others.'

'No wait, Edie. It's mine. I'll put it up.' And he took it back gently, so he didn't rip it. With another piece in place now, the jigsaw started to come alive and the six stained paper drawings displayed on the walls told a kind of story.

'Hey, Matt. I reckon that looks like Pop boiling up the billy under an awfully cloudy sky.'

'Yeah, and how do you know it's Pop?' He screwed up his face.

'Look at the mole on his forehead. It always sticks out when he really frowns.' I pointed to it closely.

'What's this?' he asked. 'Looks like a sign hanging off a post.'

'No, it's something hanging off a branch,' I whispered curiously.

'Edie, Matty! Old Pete's going,' Aunty yelled above our hushed staring. We said our farewells and he was gone into the night. One more visit over, just like the others. Pop knew that we'd follow Old Pete down to the creek. He never did say anything and besides it was school holidays. He only ever said that we weren't to bother him because he had important business to do.

As we peered through the bushes the soft rippling movement of water gave us cool thoughts. This night was a bit different from the other times. Usually he would just sit, dig the earth and hum a tune. But this night he pulled out his pencil and began to sketch. Deep in thought, he drew memories from the stars that shone above him, and as each star shone brightly, he'd ponder on its brightness and would add another thought to the picture he was drawing. Sadness wasn't what you felt for him; he was just solid.

'You're on my foot!' Matty murmured to me.

'Sshh, he heard that!' I darted my snake eyes at him. 'Let's go.' And I moved off through the bushes. 'You know, he'll never come back. Pop told us not to bother him, just watch,' I said, furiously shaking my head.

'It's like we're spies. I wonder why it's such a secret, Edie?' asked Matty.

'I don't know. Aunty and Pop are always telling us not to intrude on other folks' privacy, but look what we're doing. And Pop said it was okay!' I hunched up my shoulders.

'The old folks are losing their marbles,' Matty laughed as we made our way towards the light on the verandah.

School holidays were always fun. The sun and surf as usual beckoned my friends and me, and after the school dance Troy and Joel became our constant followers. Bronzed bodies scattered the white sand everywhere, so I didn't really need to go on a holiday. I had it all here in my own backyard.

Joel became my boyfriend. 'What a fine young man,' Aunty would say when he came calling. But I didn't know whether it was worth all the fuss. The girls stirred me up, and their teasing echoed in my mind: 'Do you roly-poly with Joely?' I couldn't wait till they had someone calling too.

'You're just sooo jealous. He's real fine and he's all mine,' I teased them back. Secretly, I loved it. He was just such a nice boy, always kind and he could make me laugh. But the best bit was he could just, only just, keep up with me when we were running. He understood my real love of flying free.

Matty had to go and visit his mum these holidays. He didn't want to go, but he missed his brothers and sisters. They were scattered too: "fostered out", Aunty said. The lot of them were coming together for a visit. His mum was getting all fixed up, and there was always the hope that they could go and live with her again.

I knew how he felt. When parts of you are missing, you get that jigsaw feeling. My mum was safe in heaven but my brothers were scattered too. They were older than me and living happily on their own, but they often visited me and then the jigsaw was complete.

'You'll have a great time, Matt,' I said, leaning on his little shoulder.

'But, Edie, it's not fair. Why couldn't they come here? It's nice and quiet here. It's safe,' he said, wiping away another lonely tear.

'Promise to write to me every day or every second day. I'll be waiting! It won't be long and you'll be back home with me!' I said, comforting the little bloke. Aunty and Pop came out with his bag and walked him to the car. *That dreaded shiny black car*, I thought when I saw it arrive, and my throat took a dive into my stomach.

I felt that strong touch of Pop's around me, and the gentle whisper, 'It'll be fine.' When Matty got into the car, Old Pete appeared mysteriously, and Pop just smiled, like he wasn't at all surprised. Old Pete patted Matty lightly on the head and handed him a gift. A pencil and a book of drawing paper. No words were spoken and the car left. There were no tears outside!

That was a difficult day, and it seemed to never end. 'Sorrow has a way of doing that,' Aunty reassured me. 'I sometimes think that life does that for us, to help us remember the happier times. You should appreciate that sorrow: it helps you grow.'

'Grow, grow, grow! I don't need to grow anymore. It makes you feel empty and always waiting for the next bad thing, and life shouldn't be like that, Aunty!' I said angrily. 'What happens if he doesn't come back? I think I'll die. I *know* I'll die!' I yelled, slamming the back door behind me. 'You're *so* mean, God!' I ran down to the creek, to my hideout.

'Edie!' I could hear her call.

'Let her go, love. Too much learning for one day,' Pop said, his words catching the end of the breeze.

As I slid down the embankment, I felt his presence and Old Pete appeared again.

'Oh, you frightened me!' I said rudely. 'I thought you'd gone. Go away! Leave me alone.' He just stood there holding yet another one of his drawings but this time he was holding it out towards me. Blinking away the tears, I stopped. Aunty's words flashed across my mind: 'Nothing is a coincidence. All is meant to just be'.

We sat for what seemed like ages, his solidness and peace seeping through to me and I slowly began to feel calm. The drawing was beautiful. It was a picture of a car speeding away with dust spitting from its wheels. It looked like Matty sitting in the back seat, but Matty was standing outside the car, watching.

'What does this mean, Old Pete?' I asked.

'No matter what we must go through, Edie, our spirit will always stay with those we love. We are all observers of our own life; it's a running movie. We won't always like what we see, but we must sometimes sit outside and just watch.'

'That's fine, but I don't want to keep on watching from the outside. Why can't I just sit on the inside and make things good, make happy things happen?' I said. He began to tell me a story that I will never forget: one that I know I will share with my children.

'The war drew many young men, full of excitement and adventure and hoping to see the world, but most importantly wanting to fight for the freedom of their country. As they left their families and friends, they knew they were doing the right thing. Making happy things happen. As you know, I was one of those young men. I went to war with your pop and two other really good mates. When we saw the shores of Gallipoli, the sense of adventure changed to real fear. There was only devastation. You were there for the good of your country, but suddenly your country wasn't there. The people's thoughts and prayers were, I'm sure, but that didn't seem to matter at that moment. Your mates became your strength and your only family.

'Well, the four of us lads became instant family, always watching out for the other. Sometimes it was just like looking at a movie, real but at the same time not real. You were outside yourself. Many times during those terrible months you'd often get this feeling of being outside and you know, beside you, it always felt like there was someone holding you up, keeping you going, and it wasn't always your mates.

'Your pop one day was in the trenches boiling the billy. It was bitter cold there. All of a sudden, gunfire. A signal came from over the sandbags telling us to get down. Exploding mud slapped our faces, and he pulled me down with him and saved my life. Within minutes another and another—then silence.'

We had our cup of tea. I suddenly thought of the drawing Old Pete gave to Matty, "the very cloudy day".

He went on, 'We moved from the trenches

to higher ground and followed a trail. We were all unsteady that day and, like I said before, standing on the outside is sometimes a good place to be. This particular day, while we walked along that trail, your pop's identification tag, called a dogtag, got caught on a branch. I was behind him and because he was tangled up, he stopped. And I stopped too!

'But just ahead of us was George, our mate. Sadly he stepped on a landmine and died. Someone on the "outside" held on to that dogtag of your pop's and saved both our lives.'

Old Pete sat still.

I thought, *that dogtag was the final bit in the picture.* And it all started to make sense now. As each picture was drawn, it pieced together their inside journey, and there was Old Pete on the outside now, looking in. After many moments he walked me back home.

How sad that so many people die without friends. Why do people who really can't find their own way lead countries and destroy those who allowed them to lead in the first place? Lost people who are always sitting on the inside. Hardly ever looking in from the outside.

And suddenly I understood what inside and outside meant.

Pop was sitting on the verandah waiting, and his smile said it all. I was glad for that simple dogtag because without it I wouldn't have had my wonderful pop or Old Pete. After that long exhausting day I slept real well.

Within a couple more days, things were back to normal. Matty was back home and looking well. He was always following me around like a lost puppy, but I didn't care.

I found out later from Mrs Irvine that Pop was an unsung hero. All the folks in town welcomed him back from the war, but because of his cultural background and the leaders of our country at that time, his service was never acknowledged.

Old Pete came to us many more times with his drawings. Matty and he would draw for hours, Old Pete showing his skills with the pencil and sharing with Matty something that I as his big sister couldn't.

As the owl hoots its message in the dark night sky, two figures crouch together and share a special friendship.

WASH THEM 'CLEAN'

School was a safe place for me and I was lucky. But I didn't really like having to go so many days in the year. Sometimes the things that I learnt never made any sense in my world, but Miss Pit said that I would store them up for future use.

We'd had Miss beady-eyed Pit for three years running. Our school was only small and Mr Jones, the principal, was like our friend and would often share in assemblies. 'We are a community here, all treated equally and each of you has your own special gifts.' He was a keen sportsman, and you could feel his caring warmth as he said good morning to you, or helped you up if you fell.

'You can run, Edie! I'll have those front-row tickets when you run for our country,' he would say with a smile, and with a quick wink he would race me across the courtyard. I always won, of course! I felt protected here at school; everyone looked out for everyone else.

The school bell was my job: I rang it to begin the day, at lunchtime, to end the day, and at my very special time on Friday afternoons, when Mr Jones took our class. He would lead us down to the back fence where we'd sit under a shady gum. He'd yarn about his adventures in an outback school he once taught at. It was another small school and his stories would take us there: the dry heat of the plains, the dust storms, the children gathering and hunting. They didn't have to sit like us at a desk; their learning was outside. It sounded like so much fun!

This day, he seemed mysteriously quiet, though, and caught up in his own thoughts.

As we sat to listen, I felt a sudden sting. I flinched and grabbed my back.

'Ouch!'

'Stop that, you fellas,' I heard Mr Jones say abruptly above their snickering. I turned round and Maggs was on top of Jed, her fist coming down on his jaw.

'Maggie, get off those boys, NOW!' Mr Jones yelled. It was on.

She didn't listen. She was a great fighter, better than most boys that I knew, and she only plugged someone if they hurt me.

'Oh, you scratch like a cat, you big girl!' I heard Jed screech.

'Lee, help me, there's something down my top. It's biting,' I squirmed and jumped madly, trying to get rid of it. Before I knew it, someone had grabbed my shirt and started jerking it up and down; finally whatever it was lost its hold.

'Oh, thanks Lee, but did you have to push me so hard?' I asked, panting to get some air.

'A bull ant?' Jed threw it away.

'Have you got a bite mark?' Lyn and Glenny asked. Mr Jones told them to go and get the first aid kit, and Lee went to fetch some water to put on my skin.

'Right, you lot! I will deal with you later. Four boys and one girl, you should be ashamed of yourselves!' Steam fumed from Mr Jones' head. Boy, I'd never seen him this mad. I thought he'd sit them away from us to cool off, but not a word was said. And, with daggers shooting from his blue eyes, he asked them to join us.

Maggie crawled close to me and whispered, 'Are you all right?' I lifted my top up and felt numb at the bottom of my spine. Mr Jones smoothed on the ointment. It stung, too.

He leant forward, 'Good shiner, Maggie.' Mr Jones was the best.

Then things cooled down.

Mr Jones began again. 'Difference,' he said. Silence fell. He went on with the story he had started much earlier.

'During the day the heat would be intolerable, and the classrooms were worse. The fans would only push out slow warm air, so I would often get my class to sit under the shade of a tree. As we sat trying to refresh our minds, we felt sad because at a daily allocated time, the children from the reserves wouldn't join us in class. We would watch as they were hosed down, lathered up and washed.

'"Wash them clean," I could hear my principal and deputy say. The children from the reserves were thought to be "different", and back then, as still today, to be dirty and not properly looked after by their parents. The principal would say to us teachers at weekly school meetings that we had to look after their hygiene and ours too. They could bring disease to our children. I felt so ashamed and so useless. I tried to fight for their rights but unfortunately a warning came about my teaching position there and future positions that I might try and apply for.

'You know, when the children were being washed, they would cry and their pain was felt by everyone watching. Those children still carry the scars, and so too do all who witnessed it. Eventually, they would join us under the tree and, funnily enough, would stir the other children that they were "appointa"—cold—while they were sitting there still hot, but, within their laughter there was a strong sense of humiliation. Nothing was said. I ask you to think about this, Year 6: should a person who is different be made to change to become like others and fit in? Or do you think that the people wanting to change them are afraid of their difference, so they act out of fear?'

Mr Jones sat quietly, and left us with these words. He asked us to pray with him, and we knew what and who for. As we went back into class, I ran to get the bell, and my back wasn't stinging anymore.

Jed asked Mr Jones could he run with me as I went to ring the bell. We didn't talk. I just knew that he was sorry for teasing me. You see, he didn't see things through the same eyes as me. His folks have taught him which side of the road to walk on; his skin is a different colour from mine and sadly what they told him made him think he was much better than me.

This time, as I ran along ringing the bell really, really loud, he ran beside me, on the same side of the road.

The memories I have of learning from Mr Jones are still with me, some sad and some happy. And Jed and his mates have gained knowledge that, as Miss Pit would say, they have stored away for future use.

WHISPERING
WINDS

'Young whippersnips! They need their mouths washed out with soap!' Aunty said angrily, as she stomped into the kitchen. It was those kids again from the other side of town.

Our town was tiny, surrounded by old gums, and lay gently across mountains that rolled down to the cool water. A lot of folk came a long way to enjoy the sea's touch. Those kids were kin and, like me, took our little town for granted.

'What's happened now?' Pop asked Aunty. I could hear them discussing things that I really wanted to know, but they thought I didn't need to know! Most times I'd stand away and listen because I had to tell Maggs anything interesting.

This day, though, I couldn't be bothered. I was hungry, so the quicker Aunty told Pop, the quicker I could eat. I knew that Aunty Junie's kids were good at cussing. They always dropped in looking for a feed. Aunty thought that they were coming over to do chores for her, but I knew better. They'd start to do the work and then leave the rest for later.

Aunty would give them whatever change she had in her purse, but this day she didn't have any because it wasn't pension week. Pop told me they got mad because Aunty didn't have any money and so they left after giving her a mouthful.

'Gwen, I don't know why you put up with it. They come here almost every week, love. Don't you think it's about time you told Junie what they're doing?' Pop said quietly. He loved my nan so much, and knew how important those kids were to her, and Aunty Junie—well, she was Aunty's sister.

The old folks' love was a mystery to me. You could see them fighting until the cows came home, yet they had an understanding, and would stick together on things. But fight? They were experts!

'No, I can't tell Junie. She'd hurt too much. She tries so hard, raising those kids on her own and all, I just can't. Maybe one day they'll be a credit to her,' came Aunty's softly spoken words.

Pop spoke loudly this time. 'Well, enough's enough! I'm going to speak to those kids. Sometimes those that hurt, no matter how young, need to hear the truth that will be whispered in their ears before too long.' And with that, the conversation ended. Pop very rarely raised his voice.

August was still cold and the sea winds sent sharp lashes that would sting your skin. Getting out of bed became a real effort and the idea of school was even worse. I would be glad when school exams were over and I could be sick. Sometimes I just needed days off to get over school. I didn't often get them because Aunty could always tell when I was foxing. But at times she would let me fox, and after a rest-fully sick day, my mind was ready for its next adventure.

But Junie's kids missed so many days. Either they were foxing sickness or just not telling Aunty Junie that they'd rather be exploring Howard's Pass, a track that led to a bush oasis only a few of us kids knew about.

This day, like many others, Dave and Blake weren't at school and because of the rain I knew they wouldn't walk. Maggie came running up to me at the school gate.

'Edie, there's a shiny car at Junie's place. What happened? Did you see them? David and the rest aren't here today. They've taken them, I can just feel it!' Maggie was in a real state, her eyes were glazed over.

'Come on, Maggs, this is real important. We'll tell Mr Jones later. I'm sure Pop will write me a note. Let's go!' I grabbed my bag, hauled it over the side fence, showing off my magnificent high-jump technique, and we were away.

It was so cold I couldn't even feel my face, but we just ran and ran. We decided to go and tell Aunty and Pop because they always knew what to do. As we approached my home, Aunty was hanging out the washing. Without blinking, she calmly told us to go inside and we did. Sitting huddled together in the parlour were Aunty Junie and her kids, fear written right across their faces.

Pop stood at the window. 'Junie, you can't keep going on like this. It's impossible to work and keep an eye on these young ones,' he said, slowly brushing the curtain to one side. Maggie and I knew this feeling well. We'd spent many a day and night hiding from those people in the shiny black car. Mr Jones our principal knew exactly what the people who arrived in the shiny car wanted. He was our friend and fortunately the car only came to school twice. When it did, Mr Jones walked and talked to the men and women, and I got an early mark—out the back gate.

Aunty was really shaking. 'Maggie, love, please go home and tell your mum what is happening. She'll know who to call.' Aunty told her to go quietly but quickly. Time seemed to stand still and silence was our friend. There were many gestures of love exchanged and silent moments full of tears in the parlour that day. Memories that I can't erase from my mind.

You see, the black shiny car did come. It was like a slow-motion movie. Every bit of pain was shared by all who watched it.

Outbursts of anger, screaming, tears. Many people came, and Aunty Junie and the kids ran and ran and ran. People chased on foot and in the car.

'They're headed towards the point!' I could hear one yell. Pop pushed me into a cupboard. The noise was too much and I couldn't move. I couldn't feel.

The Protection Board had the authority to take the children, to place them in houses that they said would be better for them. Time heals all wounds they say, but Aunty Junie and my cousins disappeared that day.

Some folks said she dived into the ocean with her children and that some of their belongings were washed up onto the shore. But the Board said they were doing what was best.

The jagged edge of the cliff face still haunts me. What folks would do to survive. Pop and Aunty sat me down to explain that fear has no boundaries but that fear can sometimes lead to hope.

Maggie's folks came that day. They knew what to do and so did others. I suppose the Protection Board didn't count on a small town's action plan to protect their own.

Aunty Junie disappeared with her kids, the townsfolk saw to that. Others spread the word that she killed herself and took the children with her, and this was enough to stop that car from coming for them again.

Aunty Junie is old now, and her choice of freedom had a high price. She never stayed long in one place, but she had her kids. Her kids are all grown up now. What happened to them has left a fear in them, but thanks to their mother they now have their freedom. And only a few people know the truth.

You can batter a people but you can't take their spirit. Mother Earth won't allow it.

TUCKSHOP

Miss Ann our tuckshop lady was always ready with an apple and a smile. No one would have guessed that she had these magical powers, especially not Maggie and I.

'Edie, could you give Miss Ann this note for me?' Miss Pit asked. Every day I seemed to be taking down a note for Miss Ann. I was so tempted to read it; just a peek wouldn't hurt, I thought.

'Just read it. No one will know,' said Maggie as she walked beside me on the way to the toilet.

'Do you think they'll know? It's like they've

got some secret or something. And I feel guilty,' I hesitated. 'But who cares!' And with that my eyes scanned the paper. It read, "Fourth from the window and sprinkle it".

Wow, what did this mean? I knew that I'd have to read each daily message to piece together all the information. Miss Pit only ever sent me and, as Maggs said, that was strange. And when I was away she didn't send a note at all.

Spring was in the air and since this was my last year of primary school, I knew time to improve my grades was running out. Aunty was not impressed with me. 'Always daydreaming about that Elvis Presley fellow! He won't improve your marks, Edie. Now put down the radio and get out your books!' Her words echoed as I listened to another blaring beat. What a dream!

Now at this time of year our school had their annual dance, and all the folks from around the area came and celebrated the season. What was I going to wear? I wondered for weeks, hoping that Aunty would buy me that dress from Miss Jessie's frock shop.

'Oh, you'd look really nice in it, Edie. Bet Joel would think so too!' Maggs crowed, with a twinkle in her eye.

'Get away! He thinks girls stink. All he notices is how well I can kick a ball. It's a football he really likes, and besides I don't like him like that,' I pouted.

'Oh you don't? So why do you always try and outrun the boys and join them in their silly footy games, hey?'

'Oh leave me alone, Maggs. What about Troy, the new boy, the one with the BIG BROWN EYES?' The words oozed from my lips.

'Come on, Edie. All I said was that he had unusual eyes,' she retorted, flicking her sun-bleached hair across my face, and jumping over every crack in the footpath. 'Besides, he can play the guitar just like Elvis.' And smiling devilishly, she started to run home. She liked him, I could tell.

I ran to catch up. 'I bet he can't dance like him, though. *Shakin' all over*,' I sang, finally keeping in step with her.

School was buzzing with excitement because the parents, after lengthy discussions, decided that the local band could play at the dance that year. At least they'd come to their senses.

'You'd think they'd forgotten what they were like when they were our age,' Sylvia whinged. 'My mum never lets me listen to the radio. That's why I have to go over to Laura's place to do my homework. She still hasn't caught on.' This was going to be the best.

Miss Pit had a surprise that day. She said Maths was about collecting and sorting, so out we went in pairs to gather anything from nature. Maggs and I teamed up. 'Reckon we get some sticks?'

'No, everyone will collect them. What about stones, Edie? I know a great place to get them.'

'Okay, I'll follow you,' I declared.

'Edie, over here.' Miss Pit's finger summoning me; once again a note for Miss Ann in her hand. 'On your way, could you please give this to Miss Ann in the tuckshop?' This time with urgency in her voice, her eyes shifting from side to side. Maggie jumping over my shoulder to catch a glimpse was annoying.

'Not again, Edie! Let's read it. Almost every day—this is weird. Maybe they're poisoning our lunches!' she whispered. Behind the old gum on the way to the tuckshop we scurried out of view.

'What's it say? What's it say? Oh no, wait, wait! Miss Ann's coming. Quick, hide it!' she said, stepping in front of me.

'Now girls, what are you up to? Come out from behind that tree. You know hiding out of class is not allowed,' Miss Ann frowned.

'Just collecting stones for Miss Pit's lesson, Miss Ann,' Maggie intercepted as she grabbed the note from my hand.

'Okay, make it quick.' And she departed as quickly as she'd appeared.

My heart in my throat, I gasped a sigh of relief. 'We're in real trouble if we get found out doing this. Hurry up and read it, Maggie,' I ordered.

The note said, "Second from the door, sprinkle". We were puzzled, but we ran and slid it under the tuckshop door. The mystery continued.

Hardly anyone went to the tuckshop because most kids brought their own lunches from home. Miss Ann's job was varied. She'd sometimes make lunches for the teachers and for special get-togethers. Different days of the week she would help kids with their reading in class, and sometimes you'd see her hammering in a nail or tending to the garden under the old snowgum tree. But I think her favourite job was making sandwiches for the old folks' home down the road.

She loved food and had such a knack for creating the most eye-catching delights, with strings of love tied to the fruit. I liked the way she would dress up the sandwiches for the old folks with funny faces that made you just want to eat them. All our class would take turns in pairs to go with her and deliver them to the folks. How their faces would light up when we arrived with the goodies! She had a special magic.

It was decided by the teachers that our class would perform at the dance that year, so we spent many hours preparing for our moment of fame. 'Psst, get away!' I threw the evil eye at Troy as he was just about to jab Maggs with another of his weapons, the dreaded ultra-sharp lead. 'I'll tell,' I whispered.

'Leave him alone,' Maggie nudged my elbow.

'You're weird to let him do that.' I darted my eyes at her.

Tap, tap, tap—Miss Pit's stick attracting our attention. 'Now to conclude our performance, we have a very talented guitarist, Troy, and accompanying him with her lovely voice will be Laura. They have been rehearsing for weeks, so please sit down and listen.'

'Oh can you believe it, Edie? Her, sing? Oh, what a dag! Look at her making googly eyes at him. It makes me want to be sick!' Maggie spoke very softly into my ear.

'Bet she sings like a frog,' I said. Their duet was good, very good in fact. 'Heart melt, Maggs, hey?' I said after we were dismissed for lunch.

This day the boys challenged the girls to a game of handball. Joel asked me to partner him, and my heart missed a beat and up flew those butterflies from the pit of my stomach. 'Okay, but I'm on the left side. It's my lucky one,' I winked. 'So we'll win!'

Maggie stood on the sideline, tongue in

cheek and rolling her head from side to side. If her eyes weren't glued into their sockets they would have rolled out, but I kept my opinion to myself.

We won. 'You're pretty good for a girl,' Joel said, giving me a wink. A wink, can you believe it? A wink! The week was almost over.

'Edie, you can ring the bell today, but, before you do, take this to the tuckshop,' Miss Pit asked. Teachers never let you know anything.

'"Children should be seen but not heard". How many times have I heard that? Just once I'd like to say "adults should be seen but not heard" because they don't know everything,' I mumbled under my breath as I left the classroom.

'You said something, Edie.' She looked right at me.

'No, no, just talking to myself.' I dashed down to the tuckshop, once again. On the way I quickly read the note and it was a similar message: "On its own, under the window, sprinkle before one". I gave the note to Miss Ann.

But this day she could see the look of intrigue in my eyes.

'Don't worry, Edie. Miss Pit and I are very good friends. These are just little notes to see how our day is going. You know, what friends share: happy words to brighten their day,' she said quietly. I smiled as I twisted my nose up and thought they were just friends.

The weekend was suddenly here and Maggie, Sylvia and Missy came over to sleep. My room was bouncing with the Brylcreem slicked through our hair. It was an Elvis special night.

'Edie, Edie, turn it down! Are you all deaf?' Pop pushed the door open.

'Sorry, Pop. What did you say?' I hollered above the music.

'I have something for you, love.' And he handed me a parcel. As I opened it my eyes couldn't believe what I was seeing. It was the dress. I wasn't normally one for dresses, but I was getting older and I needed a change.

'Oh, it's so pretty, Edie,' Missy said, and there were fingers everywhere touching its soft lacy edges.

'Oh, thanks heaps, Pop! But where did you get the money?' I was so excited!

'Never you mind. Just thank your grandmother,' his finger gently stroking my cheek. 'You'll look beautiful in it.' And he left the room.

'Now Joel will know that you're a real girl,' Maggie grinned.

'Has he asked you to the dance, Edie?' Sylvia asked.

'Don't be silly, Sylvia. We just turn up. You know the boys never dance; they just gawk,' Maggie yelled above the beat. We all laughed and started moving our hips. What a fun night.

The week before the dance had been a busy one: folks cooking food, making decorations and practice, practice, practice.

'Do you think Laura really likes Troy?' asked Maggie.

'Of course she does. Doesn't everyone just love his big brown eyes?' I joked. 'But I think he likes you best, because you can take all his torture!' She grabbed hold of my hair, yanked it, and took off. Coming towards me was Miss Pit, so I knew another message was on its way.

As I skipped down to Miss Ann, Mr Jones stopped me. 'What have you got there, Edie?' he asked.

'A message to Miss Ann from Miss Pit,' I said.

'Can I have it, please?' He held out his palm.

'No,' I blurted out, but his height made me afraid so I gave it to him.

He threw me some comforting words, 'I'll give it to Miss Ann for you.' And he walked towards the tuckshop.

There was tension in the air as I told Miss Pit about what had happened. Later during the day we had another teacher, and I knew it was to do with the note. That lady came again to our room, almost every day. She would appear outside our classroom, Miss Pit would greet her and within minutes she was back inside teaching us. Maggie slipped me a note: "Maybe she's come to talk about her child."

"No, she doesn't belong to any of the kids at this school", I wrote back. The mystery of their friendship was twisting my mind into knots. Thoughts flashed through my head. Weird notes for friends to write to one another. Maybe a secret code. Miss Ann was always digging in her vegetable garden so maybe she was making potions and putting spells on people. No, she did seem magical, but nice magical. The bell rang and it was home time.

Maggie came over because we needed to discuss with Aunty all this mystery surrounding these teachers and their notes. Hopefully she could sort it all out for us. I felt it was my fault they'd got caught. I should have put the note in my pocket, so it didn't look so obvious for Mr Jones to see.

After a lengthy talk, Aunty said, 'They're grown adults, and maybe it was just a special message they had between them. Don't worry yourselves about it. Mysteries have a way of solving themselves.'

Maggie went home for dinner, and later that night, quite late, a knock came. It was Mr Jones, looking really worried about something. I knew that it was the note! Aunty and Pop invited him in, and he asked if I could join them. He needed me to hear as well, because I was old enough. *Finally*, I thought!

It turned our that he had read the note. He said, 'The Reilly family were living on thin ice and Social Services would come to the school and check the Reilly child's bag daily, to see if he had an appropriate lunch. If he didn't he was to be extracted immediately from his family to live with another family who could care for him properly.' Mr Jones knew about these instructions. He didn't agree with them but had to abide by them.

'Luckily,' he said, 'I am blessed with staff who didn't agree either. Between Miss Pit and Miss Ann there were coded messages, delivered by you, Edie. You and the boy have the same grass roots. The notes needed to be precise as the child would move his bag wherever there was a place to hang or put it. Quick and not obvious to others. These messages would tell Miss Ann that the worker was coming soon and which bag to place a piece of fruit or a special delight in. You know, his mother always made nice lunches for him, lunches that he liked, simple fillings. But unfortunately these weren't thought to be nourishing enough for him,' he concluded.

The family was walking a constant tightrope. It had nothing to do with his appearance or home environment. Just his lunch. As simple as that. Mr Jones had come to our home to ask Aunty to talk to Mrs Reilly on the quiet, because she didn't realise that this was happening. He realised Miss Pit knew and thought that all was fine, but he wanted to keep it quiet so as not to alarm the boy, because the whole thing would affect his education. He had no idea that Miss Pit and Miss Ann had sensed the Social Services workers' anger one day and they decided to help out in their own way. Mr Jones stayed for a cup of tea and left feeling reassured that now Aunty would carry the sprinkle further.

'What did "sprinkle" mean in the note?' I asked.

'What does "sprinkle" tell you, love?' she smiled. 'Sprinkle some goodness, food, appropriate food!' she said, deep in thought. We went to bed.

The week was over quicker than it began and I didn't have to take any more notes to Miss Ann. And when she walked past me, she'd smile. Aunty fixed that.

And the dance was a success. Of course, the

old folk did more sitting than we did, but there was lots of toe tapping.

'To conclude the evening we have a very talented guitarist, Troy, and joining him to sing a familiar tune is Laura from our senior class,' announced Mr Jones. The applause thundered through the hall. After the performance, the oldies' music came on.

'Will you dance with us?' came two familiar voices from behind. Surprised, we didn't say a word. I just felt the end of Maggs's elbow nicking my ribs. And we danced for the rest of the evening.

When we were leaving I overheard Aunty say to Miss Pit and to Miss Ann, 'What exceptional talent we have at this school and how proud you both must be!' I thought, *Geez, talent does come in many forms.*

But aren't we kids lucky that some adults are seen and not heard? They just do.

HIDDEN TALENT

Applause filled the room and children stood on chairs trying to catch a glimpse of her: proud, so proud. Miss Pit smiled as a tear edged its way through her make-up. She couldn't believe how many people had come just to see her perform.

Miss Pit was a very special teacher. She walked every child through the many years of school, teaching all who came her way many life lessons and, among them, how to read and write. Our town was only small, so there wasn't much choice who taught you. We would often have a replacement teacher, and the day Miss

Pit left to pursue her hidden gift, which no one had suspected, was the day our hell began. Mr Michaels seemed nice enough to begin with, but as the weeks unfolded, so did his many regulations—and none of us escaped them.

'Now let's begin. What is an angle of ninety degrees?' he asked, all these voices shouting over each other to give the answer. 'I asked you to put your hands up. Do I continually need to repeat myself?' he bellowed, making poor Hails jump almost out of her skin. Hayley was a friend of mine, very shy and a bit nervous. She had a hearing problem but wouldn't wear her hearing aid. She'd leave it in her bag and hope that if she sat quietly enough, she wouldn't be asked to answer any questions. Any sudden loud noise she would hear gave her a fright.

'Have you a problem, miss?' he yelled directly at her face.

'No, Mr Michaels, I don't. I didn't hear what you said,' she whimpered.

'Tommy, please repeat what I just asked,' he said. Tommy repeated the question, looking straight at Hails and hoping she'd read his lips.

I felt a slight tap at the bottom of my chair and I knew Maggs was trying to pass me a note. I grabbed the note but it was for Hails who sat right beside me.

'Oh sorry, Mr Michaels, I dropped my pencil. I can be so clumsy sometimes and—' the words still tumbling from my mouth.

'Be quiet, Edie. I don't want to hear about all your goings on. You just need to get to the point,' he said. 'Now, Hayley, the answer?' His frown really did screw up his whole face just like a prune. I slipped the note into her lap, but unfortunately panic set in and she dropped it, making it obvious what I had done

'Um, um, um, something to do with the weather!' she answered.

Within a minute his almighty frame was towering over mine. 'Are you passing notes, Edie?' he demanded.

'No, Mr Michaels,' I lied. Who cared what he thought.

'Your attitude is very sad, miss. I have the note in my hand. Now, did you pass the note?' he asked again.

Oh dear. I didn't want to lie, but I didn't

want to get Hails into trouble either! 'Well, yes, but I did it to help Hayley. She didn't hear you and—' He interrupted me again before I could finish my sentence. How rude he could be! Before anyone could say a word, out came his wooden narrow stick—*wham!* Right across my desk. Hayley ran from the classroom in tears, and Maryann followed her.

'Come back, you two. Now!' And as the words spilled from his lips, his heavy boots shook the ground leading from the room. The commotion in the class grew, but what was he going to do? Hayley's mother would kill her for not wearing her aid, and he still had to come back and deal with me.

'You're in big trouble, Edie,' hollered Jacob above the noise and grinning from ear to ear. The little twerp, he had it in for me because I could out-spell him. His father was the mayor of our town, and he just loved to dob in others so he could paint a prettier picture of himself for daddy! Turmoil everywhere, books flying, rulers flicking elastic bands through the air.

'Ouch!' screamed Maggs. 'That's it, Tommy, you're gone!' And without thinking, which was typical, especially when she saw red, Maggs tackled him right into the corner of the room. It was on: the animal in everyone came out to play. Cynthia Roberts was huddled in the corner, screaming hysterically. I thought it was great. I'd never seen our class like this before. It was a day to remember. Mr Michaels sure had a way with us, and his bossiness created havoc. I wonder if he knew what kind of teacher he really was.

His shadow fell across the doorway—and there was silence. 'Sit in your allocated seats, now!' he ordered. With each of us back in our seats, we sat like a pack of cowering dogs. We licked our wounds and hoped that our punishment would be minor, like staying in after school or picking up one hundred papers each. Slowly he entered the room and closed the door. Hayley and Maryann were nowhere in sight. 'Edie, here!' he pointed to the side of his desk. *Miss Pit's desk*, I thought. I sure did miss her, especially now. I made my way to where he was pointing. You could smell his anger; beads of sweat rolled down his face. I knew now that I would really cop it and Aunty's face flashed before my eyes. She would not be impressed with me that day.

'Did you pass the note to Hayley?' he asked.

'Yes,' I quivered.

'Now this writing is not yours. Who gave you this note, Edie?' I wondered whether I should tell him it was Maggs or not.

'It's my writing, Mr Michaels,' Maggie interceded. His eyes swung across the room.

'It was my writing, Mr Michaels,' Tommy yelled out.

'No, Mr Michaels: it was my writing,' said Troy.

Luke objected. 'It's my handwriting, Mr Michaels.' Now if ever we waved a red flag at a bull, we surely did that day. I swear the beads of sweat started to rise from his chin to his forehead.

'Right. Because I can't get an honest answer, hands out,' he said quite calmly. And out came his little narrow friend, the dreaded stick. We each got six cuts. Never in all my years at school did I get punished like this. Mr Jones would have been horrified. He never agreed with smacking children in this or any other manner.

'I'm telling my dad!' howled Jacob.

'These are my class rules and I am your teacher. Respect is what is needed from you lot. Whoever has been teaching you has not been doing much of a job,' he said as each of us passed his desk and forced out an apology.

We walked home in a humiliated silence. Maggs was rubbing her shoulder.

'I think I hurt myself when I tackled Tommy,' she said.

'I think we were all hurt. What an ogre, a tall, ugly pimply monster of a teacher; that's probably why he's only a replacement teacher. Are you going to tell your mum?' I asked Maggs. 'I bet the whole class'll tell their parents. What do you think your mum will do?'

'Nothing, because in the old days they got hit with the cane, even got hit for not having their shoe laces done up properly. Can you believe it?' she said.

'I hardly ever get smacked by Pop and when I do it's no big deal because I realise I've really pushed him. But hitting to help you learn doesn't seem to make sense.' The fork in the road led us on our separate ways—wondering what school would have in store for us the following day.

'Edie, look what I have here: a postcard from Miss Pit. She's asked if you'd read it to the rest of your class,' Aunty said, handing it to me. Miss Pit was away studying drama, but she said in her card that she would be back at the beginning of next term.

'Thank goodness!' I shouted. We only had another two weeks of Mr Michaels. We had a yummy baked dinner and the chatter at the table covered all the events of the day, but Aunty and Pop were not impressed with what I told them.

'Mr Jones needs to hear about this, so I think I'll call up to the school and discuss it with him,' Aunty said.

'Probably be standing in line behind a lot of other parents,' Pop added. 'Violence definitely does not create peace. It only feeds your own anger and other people's.'

'What do you mean by that?' I asked.

'Well, love, let me explain it like this. A cake

is made up of many different ingredients, each one has its place, and in the right quantity we end up eating a cake that's really tasty. If you put in too much of one ingredient, the mixture isn't balanced right, so the cake is not what you expected. It doesn't taste nice, and that unpleasant taste stays in your mouth. Then you want to throw the cake away. And the next time the cake is made the same way, anyone offered the cake won't want a piece. Humans are like that too. Too much of one emotion affects the quality of the whole.'

'Like all the wars in the world. Only took one bad ingredient to start them,' I said.

'That's right, love. It only takes one,' he said, as he stuffed his pipe. I fell asleep to the swinging rhythms of the Glenn Miller Band. Pop was almost starting to get with it.

The bell rang and we lined up to go into class, the anxious whispers filtering down the line. Mr Michaels came out and very sternly indicated that we should follow him into the room. 'Sit down in your allocated seats, please,' he said. Five seats were vacant, and I knew why. Hayley would have by now broken out in hives as she always did when she got nervous. The other four vacant seats would have stomach aches. Tommy started to unzip his pencil case and suddenly the storm broke.

'You will not open that until I tell you to. We don't need our pencils yet,' he said firmly. All day it was like this. We couldn't move, even to wiggle a little toe. I'm sure he had x-ray vision!

We were busy doing our work and there was Mr Jones. 'Good afternoon, boys and girls,' he said in his usual friendly voice.

'Good afternoon, Mr Jones.'

'Mrs Kennedy will be working with you this afternoon. Please give her one of your very special welcomes.' And he was gone—and so was Mr Michaels. I mean: the end, no more, finally GONE from our school. We never saw him again, and Mrs Kennedy turned out to be just as nice as Miss Pit.

The last week of school came quickly and this day we discussed gifts, the gifts we receive and the ones we give. We made gifts for each other and exchanged them. The names were drawn out of a hat. I got Cynthia. How I hated her.

She was a drip, always sooky. I did try to see some good in her, but nothing surfaced, nothing obvious, anyway. We had to write a whole page about this person and what we discovered.

'Nice way to finish the term,' I whispered to Maggs. She got Troy. How lucky was that: her boyfriend! To top the exercise off, we had to spend the whole of lunch with the person we gave the gift to. Everything I did, Cynthia just sat and watched.

'Do you want to play ball?' I asked.

'No, thanks,' she said.

'What would you like to do?' I asked, kicking a stone into the air.

'Not much,' was her answer. How in the world was I going to get to know her? Everything I asked she didn't do or didn't like. She never did anything on the weekends. But I did find out that she was an only child. Her little brother died when he was four years old of a blood disease, and that was sad. Her family just stayed home all the time.

'What's that you're fiddling with?' I asked, trying to look over her shoulder.

'Nothing,' she turned her back on me.

'Come on, what is it?' I reached for her closed hand. As she opened it, there in her palm was a little red star.

'That's really pretty. Can I hold it?'

'Okay, but you must promise to hold it for only a second,' she said, wiping it across the palm of my hand.

'Who gave it to you? Does it stick?' I tried to stick it on my dress.

'No, it's a little present from my brother.' And with that she took it from me. 'I find them all the time. He sends them to me from heaven,' she said with a smile on her face.

'Wow, that's weird,' I said, looking above to the clouds. 'How does he do that?'

'I don't know, but I always find them and I just know he's happy and safe and that he is looking after me. I used to take little packets of stars and give them to him in hospital.' And then the bell rang again. I stood there, still cloud gazing.

'Come on, Edie. Stop dreaming,' Maggie said, racing past and pushing me into line. I sat that afternoon and wrote about Cynthia's gift. I wrote two whole pages, and that was a miracle for me. Her gift was that she believed. I got an 'A' for my work.

Mrs Kennedy read my story to the class. She told us that we all had gifts: some that we see; others we don't or don't know about yet—they were to come. She was a friend of Miss Pit's, she said. 'Sometimes a gift is a dream that we secretly have and tell no one. Sometimes it takes a simple turn of events like breaking your ankle and someone has no alternative but to replace you. This is what happened with Miss Pit and me. I was rehearsing for our local theatre group one Friday evening. Miss Pit drove me because my car broke down and she said she'd wait till it finished. I fell and broke my ankle and the rest is history. Miss Pit was our only audience. She very shyly agreed to replace me and out of the cocoon, unfolding her wings, flew the most beautiful butterfly. That's when she realised that her secret dream had become a gift for all of us to share.' Mrs Kennedy smiled, closed her books, erased the board and gave us all an early mark to start our holidays.

Teachers come all sorts of ways: some stand still, some walk and some fly...

To Mum
You truly are the wind beneath my wings.
Love
   Frances x

Fran Dobbie talks and laughs all the time, but when she was asked to say something about herself, she was stumped. After days of talking and writing about everything else, this is what she said:

'Because I hated school but love children and because I'm a big kid myself, I decided as an adult that I would venture into the playground once again and become a teacher—hoping that I could encourage others to want to go to school. I got my teaching degree, surprised myself and passed with a distinction, suddenly realising that anything is possible if you have a dream and passion.

I love the fun I have with the kids. We have a campsite so that the children can appreciate nature at first hand. And we do tai-chi every morning, so that their day begins with balance; mine too!

My spirituality is very important to me: the connection with the earth and those who walk it constantly inspires me to search, share and enjoy. My people are English (Dad) and Australian with Aboriginal descent (Mum)—the Yuni tribe on the south coast of New South Wales.

I live in a country town outside Sydney and have two boys. What fun they are and what a challenge they can be! I don't like housework, ironing or cooking but love entertaining my friends and having a good laugh. I love to walk with my dog, camping, 4wd and yoga.

That's it: I can't think of anything else.'